Fiancé for Hire

Men for Hire

Sharon C. Cooper

Amaris Publishing LLC

Fiancé for Hire

By
Sharon C. Cooper

ISBN: 978-1-946172-47-1
Paperback

Tamara (pronounced Tah-Mare-Ah) Kingsby.
Gone but never forgotten. RIH
5/10/2023

* * *

And to my sister, Loretta, you're the best!
Love you!

Chapter One

"**Y**ou need a man."

Antika Wilcox snorted at her best friend's words and placed the pot roast and potatoes in the center of the glass kitchen table.

"Been there. Done that. It didn't end well—remember? Now, grab that salad so that we can eat."

She and Tamera had been friends since kindergarten and had dinner together once a week, usually on the weekend. It was a rare occasion that Antika wasn't traveling for work. But recently, her travel schedule had been cut back, and no one was more thrilled than her.

"I'm serious about you needing a man," Tamera said, circling back to the conversation as she set the glass bowl of tossed salad on the table. "Now that you and ol' what's-his-name have parted ways, you need a date for my birthday party. It's the big 4-0, and I'm doing it *big*. So I don't want my best friend to be there by herself, not having a good time."

Inwardly, Antika cringed. She was so sick of men, especially since she couldn't seem to pick a good one. Her heart had

1

been crushed one too many times, and she couldn't put herself back out there again. She'd rather be alone than keep putting up with the crap that the male species dished out.

It all started nineteen years ago when she was twenty and married her college sweetheart. *Big* mistake. Patrick-The-Wimp—the name that Tamera had given him—ended up dumping her for his friend's sister.

Two years...

For two years of marriage, Antika had put up with his arrogance, his selfishness, and she had even tolerated his controlling nature. They'd been too young to get married, but back then, she thought she was in love. He was the big man on campus, and he had chosen her to be his woman.

In the end, the emotional pain he'd caused, combined with his betrayal, had broken something inside of her.

Even now, Antika felt sick thinking about that time in her life. Little had she known that adulting was a lot harder than she had counted on. Combine that with a self-absorbed husband who didn't know how to love her—or just didn't give a damn—and it was a recipe for divorce.

Of course, when she was twenty-two and made it to the WNBA, Patrick came crawling back, telling her that he'd been a fool to ever let her go. He wanted them to try again. Before they got married, they both imagined her as a WNBA superstar, living large and being in the public's eye. Patrick had wanted the potential lifestyle more for himself than for her.

So when he came back around when she entered the league, Antika literally laughed in his face. Playing professional basketball—her dream job—would've been sweet revenge against him. Unfortunately, she tore her ACL at the end of her first season.

That was the end of her professional basketball career.

Since then, she managed to attract one loser after another,

and she was done. If it meant being single for the rest of her life to keep her sanity, so be it. That was precisely what she planned to do.

"I don't need—nor do I want—a date," she said as she loaded her plate with food. "Oh, shoot, let me open a bottle of wine. How about a cabernet sauvignon?"

"I'd never say no to any type of wine. Why do you think I come over here so much for dinner? You always have the best vino."

As a district manager for Bottle Brigade Wine & Spirits distributor, Antika knew her wines and her collection was impressive, if she said so herself. She'd been with the company for fifteen years and had honed her palate after tasting hundreds of different wines.

"I have an idea for your man problem," Tamera said as she accepted the glass of wine, and Antika set the bottle on the table.

"I don't have a man problem, but I'm starting to have a best friend problem."

Tamera laughed. "Whatever. Hear me out. I heard about this company where you can hire men for anything from changing a light bulb to fixing your plumbing. I'm talking about kitchen/bathroom plumbing—not the euphemism for sexing you up."

Antika sputtered a laugh, causing some of her wine to dribble down her chin. She continued chuckling as she dabbed at her face with a napkin.

"I'm serious," Tamera continued. "If you need an escort, someone to be your plus-one at parties, or even pretend to be your boyfriend or your husband, this organization promises to have everything you need."

Antika shook her head as her friend pulled up the company's website on her cell phone and handed it to Antika.

Copperplate script lettering across the top of the screen read At Your Service. The website was tastefully done in bold colors and appeared straightforward and businesslike. Scanning the content, she had to admit that it was an interesting concept, but she didn't see what the men they employed looked like.

The website also informed readers that anyone interested in utilizing their services would have to fill out the company's detailed questionnaire and then visit their office for a face-to-face in-depth interview.

Antika placed the phone down next to her friend's plate. "No," she said simply. "I would never go through a service to find a man."

Never might've been a strong word, but in this case, Antika knew there was no way she'd hire an escort.

And why should she? She didn't need a man.

* * *

Days later, Antika tossed her favorite pen onto the desk and rocked back in her office chair. She hated meetings, and today had been loaded with them. She had one more to attend.

Every other Wednesday, the directors met with the big bosses, and those gatherings were mentally draining.

But worse than that, she'd have to spend those two hours with Edward—her ex-boyfriend—sitting at the table.

Antika started to rub her eyes but stopped herself just in time. She rarely wore eye makeup, but today was different. Shamelessly, she wanted to look good for Edward.

Not that she wanted him back. No, that was definitely not the case.

She wanted to show him that her life was better without

him. What better way to demonstrate that than looking her best at work?

That was also why she'd worn a dusty blue wrap dress that stopped above her knees and had gorgeous bell sleeves. The matching high heels were sexy; too bad they were so uncomfortable.

Still, she felt beautiful. More so than she did when she wore her usual conservative pantsuits to work. Tamera had been on her about upping her wardrobe game, especially since Douchebag Edward—Tamera's words—thought that she, Antika, was sitting at home eating bon bons and pining over him.

She wasn't.

Well, not exactly.

No, she hadn't been out much since they broke up, but it wasn't because she was miserable without him. It had everything to do with the fact that she was sick of men, especially him.

A knock sounded on her door, and Antika sat forward. "Come in," she called out.

The door swung open, and her administrative assistant stuck her head in. "Just wanted to remind you about your meeting that starts in fifteen minutes. They moved it to the tasting room."

Antika sighed. That meant that they had company—most likely a new client who probably bought wine samples. "Okay, thanks, Megan."

"No problem." Megan backed up, closing the door behind her.

Antika opened the bottom desk drawer and removed her large purse. After checking her makeup and reapplying her tinted lip gloss, she headed to the tasting room. All was fine until she spotted Edward flirting with one of the front desk secretaries.

The way the woman was batting her long fake eyelashes and touching his arm, it was safe to say they were...friendly. Which shouldn't be a surprise. It seemed Edward was making his way around to every female in the office.

Antika hated that she'd allowed herself to be one of them.

They must've heard her footsteps drawing closer because they jumped apart. The moment Edward saw Antika, that smug smile of his—the one that grated on her nerves—spread across his lips.

How the heck had she ever been attracted to him?

Sure, he was good-looking in a young Malik Yoba kind of way when he played J.C. on *New York Undercover*. Tall, dark, with sexy bedroom eyes and a body designed for bear hugs, but still...Edward was an arrogant asshole. It frustrated her that she had wasted months of her valuable time with the jerk.

"Hello, Antika. If you're heading to the meeting, I'll walk with you," he said, winking at the secretary before pushing away from the counter that she was sitting behind.

"Don't bother. I didn't mean to interrupt your next conquest," Antika said, picking up speed in hopes that he'd get the message. Of course he didn't. She should've ignored him.

"You didn't interrupt anything, and Latoria is not my next conquest. We're just...hanging."

"Either way, I feel sorry for her." Antika felt bad for any woman who'd end up with the narcissistic sleazebag.

Edward laughed and the guttural sound was like having thousands of ants skittering across her skin. Then he *tsked*. "Poor Antika. Jealousy doesn't look good on you. I guess that means that you're still a bitter spinster with no hopes of ever finding someone whose interest you can keep."

Antika almost clutched her chest at the comment. It hit her

right in the heart, and it was a struggle to keep her head held high as she walked a little faster. Leave it to him to touch on one of her insecurities.

"I see you dressed up today. Nice try hiding those thick thighs and that belly roll," he continued, smirking as he shook his head. "Don't you get tired of your thighs rubbing together and your stomach jiggling?"

Bam! Another direct hit.

Antika was glad they were the only ones in the hallway as she struggled to keep her composure. But there was no way in hell she'd let him see how his words affected her. Instead, she put on a smile that she hoped appeared real and slowed her steps.

"Oh, Edward. Don't you ever get tired of being a pompous, misogynistic asshole? It's *really* not a good look," she whispered, disgust in her tone. Then she picked up speed as her heart pounded angrily against her rib cage.

Edward chuckled. "Ahh, come on, Antika. I'm kidding...but are you lashing out because you don't have a man? I guess that means you'll be all alone for Battle Brigade's All-Star Celebration. What a shame," he said in mock sympathy when he caught up to her.

The All-Star Celebration, which would take place in a few weeks, was being hosted by the owners of the company. They wanted to do something to reward the management team for landing three back-to-back million-dollar contracts within a two-month period.

At first, Antika had been looking forward to the event. It wasn't every day that the company threw a spectacular gala for them. The recognition was well deserved, since she and the others had worked their butts off to land those contracts. They had earned that celebration, the financial bonus that came with it, and the recognition. The owners generously extended the offer for the honorees to bring their significant others.

Leave it to Edward to squash her excitement.

He shook his head and *tsk*ed again. "I heard there will be live music, the best meal money can buy, and champagne flowing all night. Too bad you'll be attending alone."

Something inside of Antika snapped. She stopped abruptly and so did he.

Instead of giving him the satisfaction of knowing he'd gotten to her, Antika laughed, even though laughing was the last thing she felt like doing. She couldn't let him win this round.

Stepping closer to him, a burst of pleasure filled her when he stiffened.

"Edward, Edward, Edward," she said, fingering one of the buttons on his dress shirt. "Since you're so concerned about my personal life, you really should keep up. I have a lover, and he's way more of a man than you'll ever be."

She dropped her hand and straightened her shoulders. "Now, if you'll excuse me. I have a meeting to get to." She turned and sauntered off.

Damn it. Tamera was right.

I need a man.

Chapter Two

"So let me get this straight. You want to assign me to one of your clients, and she's waiting in your office?"

Drevon Ross stared at his aunt, waiting for her to say *just kidding*, but those words never came.

Viola Ross was serious.

He was back in Atlanta for less than a week and already people were trying to hog his time. Of course, it was mostly his family and closest friends who thought just because they wanted him to do something for them, he'd automatically say *yes*.

Not today.

Drevon had been in Europe for the last four months on a couple of modeling assignments and a small acting role. He loved traveling and his profession had given him an opportunity to see the world.

Modeling might not have been his first choice of careers, but it afforded him more opportunities than he could ever have dreamed. All those opportunities were getting him closer to his ultimate goal—producing a big-budget film. Part of the reason

9

he returned to Atlanta was to meet with a few investors—not to be at his family's beck and call.

"Don't say no," his aunt said in a rush. "You're going to thank me for this."

"I highly doubt that," he said dryly, running his hand over the scruff on his cheeks and chin.

After his last assignment, he'd started growing out his beard. That was one of many things he was happy that he could now do since he wouldn't be taking on any modeling assignments for a while. The beard also helped with people failing to recognize him right away when he was out in public.

"Aunt Vi, I assumed you were joking. Since you're not, you need to find someone else. I'm not interested. I'm not some piece of meat that you can put on display, or some man-candy for you to distribute to women."

"Oh, hush," she said, chuckling. "I know you're a catch, which is why you'll be perfect for this young lady. She's a few years older than you, but—"

"No," he said, growing less interested by the minute.

When his aunt had left him a message saying that she needed him to come by the office as soon as possible, he had no idea what to expect. She'd sounded a bit ominous, and on his way there, Drevon had tried calling her cell phone numerous times. The calls had gone straight to voicemail.

Now he knew why.

She wanted to blindside him with this request.

He shook his head. "No way. I'm not letting you pimp me out."

His aunt and uncle were the CEO and CFO, respectively, of At Your Service, but this was the first time she had tried anything like this.

"Sweetie, it's not like that. This month we have been

slammed with requests for escorts That is a good thing, but it's put us in a bind."

Sighing, she reminded him that successful women were struggling to find men to meet their various needs, such as doing repairs around the house. She saw more of a need when it came to those same women needing a companion for an event or two—which was the case in this situation.

After being successful in matching a few family members, Viola realized she could make a living at doing something that she was a natural in—matchmaking. She was good at pairing women to the company's escorts. To her credit, his aunt had a ton of success matching her siblings and some of her in-laws—and now perfect strangers.

"I honestly don't have anyone available at the moment who fits her requirements—except for you. Since you're in town and taking time off, I thought you'd be perfect for this assignment. You've already been vetted. So if you'll agree, I'll be able to go ahead and match the two of you."

The organization was a single woman's dream. It usually had a man for anything a woman could possibly need, but technically Drevon hadn't signed on to be one of his aunt's *men*. She had roped him into completing the online profile supposedly to test out the company's software. Drevon assumed she had deleted the information, but apparently not.

Not only had she not deleted it, but it sounded like she had updated it.

"Let's go to my office. You can meet the woman face-to-face," his aunt continued. "She's beautiful, successful, well-connected, and this is the first time that she's using our services. I couldn't tell her we didn't have anyone for her."

"Fine, I'll tell her." Drevon started for the door, but his aunt stopped him with a hand on his arm.

"You will do no such thing."

"Aunt Vi, I would normally be willing to help you out, but now is not a good time. I came back to Atlanta to regroup. Not to be someone's paid escort."

"It wouldn't be like that. She mainly needs a friend—a male friend who can attend a few events with her, and that's all. Trust me when I tell you she's amazing. She's not the type of woman you usually date. This woman is not only beautiful, but she's smart, carries herself like a lady, and she has a successful career."

Drevon chuckled under his breath. He knew there was a dig somewhere in that statement about his dating life, but he didn't take it personally.

Yes, he'd dated his share of gorgeous yet shallow women. It wasn't always by choice, but he couldn't help that those were the types of women who threw themselves at him. And since he hadn't been looking for anything serious, just a good time, he usually played along.

That was his other reason for taking time off and returning home.

He needed a break—time to evaluate his life and determine whether he was on the right track with his future goals. Mainly, he needed to make some changes in his life.

Specifically, his personal life.

"Aunt Vi, I—"

"Come on, Dre. Don't say no. I know Kendall did a number on you, but this is your chance to forget about her and have a little fun."

Drevon gritted his teeth at the mention of his ex. His chest heaved just thinking about Kendall Monroe, an award-winning actress he'd dated for months.

Heat spread through his body as a sudden bout of anger simmered in his chest. Her antics, lies, and blatant disrespect toward him could've cost him everything, including his freedom. He would never forgive her.

"I've never asked you for a favor before," his aunt said, "but I need your help on this one."

Drevon released a long breath and was slow to speak as he struggled to reel in his frustration. There wasn't much he wouldn't do for his aunt, but this...

"Why me? Why do you need me to escort this woman? I'm trying to lay low, especially after that mess with Kendall."

"Honey, I understand," she said, patting his arm. "But what better way to get over one woman than by helping another one out? Especially one who only wants you for a couple of events."

Drevon sighed. He couldn't believe that he was considering doing this.

He glanced down at his attire. He was wearing a designer black-and-white printed zip-placket polo with black walking shorts patterned identically to the shirt. The silver jewelry around his neck and wrist, along with black boat shoes, set off the outfit.

Though the ensemble could be considered casual-dressy to some, he wasn't dressed to meet a potential client.

"You look perfect," his aunt said as if reading his mind. She stood and nodded toward the door. "Come on. I'll introduce you."

Drevon grumbled under his breath. "Let me make a quick phone call, and I'll be there shortly."

Viola narrowed her eyes. "Don't even think about sneaking out of here, because I'll find you." With that she left, closing the door behind her.

What the hell was he doing?

Had his life really come to this—a paid escort?

Chapter Three

Ntika paced the length of Mrs. Ross's office, an average-sized space that was beautifully decorated. With the calming gray wall color, and the comfortable looking sofa and reading chair in the far corner, Antika should've been soaking up the peacefulness of the space.

Instead, she couldn't stop asking herself: *What the hell was I thinking signing up for At Your Service?*

She huffed out a weary breath and shook her head. Her footsteps might've been quiet against the plush carpet, but her heart was pounding loud enough to be heard down the hall. She wasn't a hasty person. Hell, she overthought everything in her life—but she had been too quick to jump on the idea of hiring a man to be her date.

I'm paying someone to go out with me.

"How pathetic is that?" she mumbled, then growled aloud into the quietness of the room.

She had completed the questionnaire the night before, and it had been a simple process. The questions centered around basic details like her age, height, gender preference, annual income, and level of education.

The last part of the questionnaire contained questions that made her think long and hard before responding. They delved deeper into her personality, asking questions that she never thought about, such as: How did you handle your last failure? What is your first memory of yourself as a child? What would your last meal be?

She assumed the responses would determine who in their database might be compatible with her. But the unfortunate thing about her responses to the questions was, if she was asked the same questions on a different day, her answers would probably be different. They were subjective questions about her feelings on a topic, or her attitude regarding a subject.

Despite all the time it took to complete the questionnaire, Antika was having second thoughts about it all.

"I can't do it. I can't go through with it," she admitted to herself, then moved to the sofa where'd she'd been sitting, and grabbed her handbag.

Unfortunately, she'd always been one of those people who cared what others thought of her. What would people think if they found out that she hired someone to be her plus-one?

Yet, here she was, hiring a man to escort her to a few events. All because she didn't want family, friends, and her stupid ex-boyfriend—Edward—to think that she was too pathetic to get a date.

"So much for living on my own terms," she murmured.

Before Antika could leave the office, the door flew open, startling her.

"I am so sorry for the delay," Mrs. Ross said as she blew into the room and moved around to the other side of her desk. "Please forgive me. I needed to handle a situation that couldn't wait. Now, where were we?"

"Actually, I changed my mind," Antika said as she slipped her purse strap onto her shoulder. "I'm sorry for any inconvenience this might cause, but I no longer need your services."

"Oh, there you are," Mrs. Ross interrupted while glancing around Antika.

Antika turned to find a tall, handsome man standing in the doorway. He was all matchy-matchy in an ugly outfit, but it looked as if it had been tailored specifically for his physique. Considering how well-groomed and put together he was, he looked as if he had just finished a photo shoot for a men's fashion magazine.

She hoped this wasn't the guy Mrs. Ross was trying to set her up with. He was good-looking with skin the color of honey, and a five o'clock shadow covering his cheeks and chin. Actually, he looked familiar, but he was everything she didn't want in a man. Preppy. Tidy. A slave to fashion, and he was too damn pretty.

Antika preferred her men thick, dark, and rugged. This guy might've been a little muscular, but he was too nerdy-looking for her. Well, maybe not nerdy. He did kind of give off Drake— the singer—vibes with his swag, dark eyes, and facial hair. Still, he was too...*polished*.

Nope. Not my type.

He did have one thing going for him—he was tall. At five-eleven in her bare feet, she preferred men who were at least six-three or taller, and this guy fit the bill.

But that was it.

"He's not my type," Antika blurted before she could pull the words back.

"What the hell?" the man barked, and a shiver skittered over Annika's skin.

Good Lord. That voice.

That deep, sexy, make-you-want-to-drop-your-panties voice surged through her, sending shock waves to every nerve in her body.

Mentally, Antika shook herself. *I'm not interested. I'm not interested.*

So what if his voice should be used to read sex scenes aloud in every romance novel...

It didn't matter.

She wasn't interested.

At least that's what she kept telling herself.

"I'm sorry, but you're not what I asked for," Antika continued and waved her hand up and down, gesturing at his body. "You're tall, but that's it. Nothing else matches my criteria."

"Well, excuse the hell out of me, lady. Do you know who I am?" he asked, his voice going even deeper as he scowled at her.

Mrs. Ross leaped from her chair and moved around to the front of the desk. "Ms. Wilcox," she said, her tone soothing. "May I call you Antika?"

Antika nodded, wondering again why she had let Tamera talk her into this foolishness. No—it was actually because of Edward. Antika had let his silly words get to her. So this was all on her.

"I know Drevon might not be exactly what you requested, but I assure you that he is perfect for you," Mrs. Ross said, then raised her hands in a placating gesture. "I mean, he's the perfect escort for what you're looking for. Trust me, dear. The men that work with our agency are the most eligible bachelors in Atlanta; perhaps in the entire country. In addition to that, I've been credited with matching couples since before you were born. I assure you that I'm very good at what I do, and my success rate is stellar."

"Hey, if she doesn't need a man, cool. I'm out of here," the guy said, and once again his voice—deep and raspy—rocked Antika from the top of her head to the soles of her feet.

Goodness. When it came to distinct, soul-stirring voices like Barry White, James Earl Jones, and even Morgan Freeman, this man was absolutely in their league.

Still, it wasn't enough for Antika to change her mind.

He turned for the door, but Mrs. Ross rushed to block his path.

"Don't leave the building," she told him. "Wait for me in the other room."

He stared at the woman for the longest time, then dropped his shoulders and gave a slight nod.

Antika sensed a silent conversation going on between them, but couldn't be sure. Maybe he had worked for the woman long enough to where they could communicate without words.

It didn't matter. She was no longer interested in being matched.

"Antika, you wouldn't have come here if you didn't want a handsome man on your arm to attend a few events with you," Mrs. Ross said after the man left. "You've already done the hard part—completing the personal profile. Why not give me a chance to show you how good I am at what I do?"

Antika shook her head, willing herself not to fall for this woman's persuasiveness and charm. "I can't. I have never been so uncomfortable in all my life. I don't do this—I don't buy or hire guys to go out with me."

"Honey, don't look at it like that. You're hiring *me* to provide a service for you. That's all it is. Granted, on the surface, Drevon doesn't look like the man you had in mind, but I assure you he's a perfect fit. Give him a chance."

Antika released a shaky sigh. "I don't know. This is so not like me. I—"

"Give *me* a chance. If you don't enjoy Drevon's company, I'll refund your money one hundred percent."

After a long hesitation, Antika started to say *no thanks.*

Instead, for some reason, she said, "Let me think about it."

Chapter Four

The moment Tamera opened her apartment door, Antika shoved past her and headed to the living room. She plopped down on the black cushiony sofa and huffed out a sigh.

Who hires a man to go out with her? This wasn't her style. She had too much integrity to stoop to this level, and no way could she lie about having a boyfriend or a date—or whatever the heck the guy was going to be to her.

But now she had another problem.

Her possible fake date was dominating her thoughts. Despite telling him and Mrs. Ross that he wasn't her type, Antika was shamelessly curious about him...and that voice.

"Well, come on in and make yourself comfortable," Tamera cracked, and Antika glanced over her shoulder at her friend, who was still standing at the door with a hand on her hip. She slammed it shut. "To what do I owe the pleasure of this unexpected, yet wonderful surprise visit?"

"Have you ever decided to do something and then later think—*What the hell was I thinking?*" Antika asked. "You realize that you didn't think the situation through, and then you start imagining how your decision can backfire in so many ways. Well, I did it. I went to that man-for-sale agency that you recommended, and I'm asking myself—why do I always let you talk me into crap like this?"

"Wait." Tamera rushed to the sofa and plopped down. "You went to At Your Service? I can't believe it. How was it? Did you see any cute men? Tell me everything, and *please* tell me you have a picture of the guy who'll be your temporary man."

Antika dug through the side pocket of her purse for her cell phone. "He is so not my type. I requested a dark chocolate, tall, rugged man, and I ended up with this guy."

Tamera studied the photo. "What are you talking about? This guy is a cutie. He actually looks like that model—Drevon Ross."

Antika stared at her friend. "Hold up. You know that guy?"

"No, I said he looks like—"

"His name *is* Drevon Ross!" Antika shrieked, then leaped to her feet and started pacing in front of the sofa. "No way it can be the same guy, but... he's the model? Like—like the famous model? Why didn't they tell me? I assumed he was some regular Joe Blow in their database."

"Wait, I'm confused." Tamera stood and shuffled through the magazines on the cocktail table before lifting one and turning the front cover to Antika.

Antika stared at it, and her heart slammed against her chest. The exquisite human being on the cover wearing a black suit with a black turtleneck and silver jewelry was mouthwatering gorgeous.

"Are you telling me that cutie-pie Drevon Ross is the person they hooked you up with? The person who'll be your date for my birthday party next weekend? The person you'll be taking to your company's gala?"

Antika covered her face with her hands and growled. "Oh. My. God. This just keeps getting worse. Why did I let you talk me into this? I can't go out with a famous model." She dropped her hands and looked at her friend. "I especially can't take him to the company's event. They'll never believe someone like him would be involved with someone like me."

Tamera was still standing in front of her with wide eyes and her mouth hanging open. "How in the world did you get hooked up with him? Is he as gorgeous in person as he is on magazines and television?"

"He looks like some...some pretty boy. You know I don't do pretty boys. I prefer tall, dark, and rugged. Not cute, conservative, and...*fine*."

"Whoa! My best friend is hooked up with Drevon Frickin' Ross! Wait until I tell everybody!" She squealed and did a happy dance, rolling her shoulders and rocking her hips to some silent beat playing inside her head.

"I'll have a celebrity at my party, and it is going to be lit! Oh, I know. See if he'll bring a couple of his famous peeps. I heard he was good friends with Michael B. Jordan and—"

"Stop!" Antika screamed before she got Tamera's attention. "You are *not* to say a word to anyone about this. I'm not sure I'm going through with this arrangement. I was a nervous wreck by the time I left the place. There's no way I'll be able to go through with this."

Tamera set the magazine on the table and stood in front of Antika, gripping her shoulders, and forcing Antika to look at her.

"If you cancel on Drevon before I get to meet him, I will never speak to you again. I mean it!" she snapped. "Now, sit your ass down and let me talk some sense into you."

Antika huffed out a sigh and fell back onto the sofa as she tuned out Tamera. Antika didn't need to be talked into anything. She had already made up her mind—she couldn't do it. She shouldn't have let Mrs. Ross set her up in the first place.

And then there was Drevon. A famous model.

In her mind, she replayed everything that she'd said to him in Mrs. Ross's office and groaned. Normally, she wasn't so rude.

He probably thinks I'm a total whack job. Especially since she was the one who went looking for a date, and then had the nerve to complain that he wasn't what she'd wanted. He wasn't her type.

"Gawd! I can't believe I let Mrs. Ross almost talk me into going out with him. She insisted that we would be perfect together, and—"

"Mrs. Ross?" Tamera said slowly as she sat next to Antika. "Mrs. Ross...like in his *mother*? She works at the company?"

Antika froze. *Ross. Drevon Ross.* "Ahh, hell."

How did I not catch that?

"Wait. I'm having trouble keeping up," Tamera said. "His mother paired you guys? Dang, you actually met his mother. Most women don't meet the potential in-laws until long after they've been dating. And you—"

"We're not dating," Antika growled as she searched her memory trying to recall if Mrs. Ross said anything about Drevon being her son. "No way was that his mother. It couldn't have been. They didn't look anything alike, and they didn't act like mother and son, though they were friendly. I don't think she's his mother," Antika said quietly, but didn't know for sure.

"Well, then they must be related somehow. That's too much of a coincident that he'd have the same last name as the woman who owns the company." Tamera tapped her fingers against the arm of the sofa. "Just think, you should be flattered.

If this woman is his mother or a close relative, she must've been really impressed by you to set you two up."

"Don't you think that's a little creepy?" Antika said, laying her head against the sofa as she stared at the ceiling. "Why would he agree to be in their database? Surely a supermodel wouldn't need to be escorting women."

"Nah, that brother doesn't have problems getting dates. I'm sure there are plenty of women dropping their panties for him. Which reminds me...he had a bad breakup like eight or nine months ago. He was dating that actress, Kendall Monroe, and things didn't end well. I think he even got arrested, but it turned out that she had lied and then, trying to make herself look like the victim, she warned women to stay away from him. I think Drevon ended up suing her for defamation of character or something."

Oh, yeah, this just keeps getting better, Antika thought.

Antika listened as Tamera told her that before that incident, there was never any negative publicity regarding him. That he did a lot of charity work and collaborated on numerous projects with people in the entertainment industry, while the actress was always caught up in some drama. According to rumors, the two had dated for months, and she was mad that he didn't want to marry her. She accused him of having commitment issues and had even attacked his manhood.

"Considering how successful she is, I don't understand why she's always going after these guys. She's been seen with so many A-list actors, and it seems the relationships always end badly," Tamera explained. "Clearly, she's the one with the problem since she's the common denominator in the situations."

Antika sighed. "I don't want any drama in my life, and this guy sounds like he's surrounded by drama. I think it'll be best if I cancel my request with At Your Service."

"Nope. I'm not letting you do that. Think about Edward. Do you really want to go to your work event by yourself while your ex is there with some hoochie? Because I doubt he'll show up alone," Tamera said with confidence. "And it would be sweet revenge if you were there with one of the hottest guys on the face of the planet."

She had a point, but Antika needed to think about all of this.

Then again, what would it be like to go out with a famous model?

Chapter Five

Devon left his Range Rover with the valet and jogged up the few stairs to Canoe, one of his favorite restaurants located in Vinings—a neighborhood in Atlanta along the banks of the Chattahoochee River. It was a good thing he had made a reservation, because based on the number of cars in the lot, the place was packed.

He was meeting Antika Wilcox for lunch.

To say she had shocked him when she called last night and asked him to meet her for lunch would be an understatement. He had considered declining since he planned to tell his aunt he couldn't take the assignment—mainly because he and Antika's initial encounter the day before hadn't gone well.

Besides that, the idea of being someone's hired date didn't appeal to him.

But his curiosity had gotten the best of him. He hadn't stopped thinking about Antika since walking out of his aunt's office. So much so, that he had reviewed her profile and intake form that his aunt had given him. He could admit that she was a nice-looking woman, and he was physically attracted to her.

But the fact that she used to play professional basketball had piqued his interest.

"Good afternoon, welcome to Canoe," the hostess greeted as he entered the restaurant. "Do you have a reservation?"

He removed his sunglasses, and though her bright smile was still plastered on her pink lips, her perfectly arched eyebrows dipped slightly into a frown. Drevon recognized the look. She was trying to figure out where she knew him from.

"Yes, I do. It should be under Ross," he said, and it was as if a lightbulb went on inside her head, and then her eyebrows shot up.

"Ahh, yes, Mr. Ross. Welcome!" Her smile broadened as she flipped her long auburn hair over one shoulder as she glanced at the computer screen in front of her. "Has your guest arrived yet?"

"No. I'm a little early, but she should be here shortly." He didn't know that for sure, but he hoped Antika wasn't one of those women who liked to be *fashionably* late. Or worse—one who would stand him up.

"No problem. If you'd like, I can seat you now and then show your guest to the table once she arrives."

"That sounds good." Drevon slipped his aviator sunglasses back on and followed the woman into the main dining room.

Once he was seated near the window, he looked out and admired the nice view—lush flowers and trees in a park-like setting and the peaceful Chattahoochee River as the backdrop. It was just as nice inside. The upscale restaurant, with a ceiling shaped like a canoe, tables covered with white tablecloths, and soft jazz playing in the background, had a warm and inviting ambiance. That, along with the excellent food, was why he had suggested the place.

As Drevon glanced around, a few women were staring at him. One even nodded and smiled, and he returned the gesture. Used to the attention, he took it in stride and was glad none of them approached the table. He hated when that happened. Most people showed respect when it came to letting him eat in peace, but there had been a few bold women over the years who didn't give a damn.

Lifting his menu from the table, he skimmed it while wondering if Antika would show up. Especially since she claimed he wasn't what she wanted. He wasn't her type.

A smile spread across his face. He had never heard those words come out of a woman's mouth before—*ever*. Knowing that he wasn't her type gave him another reason to say yes to lunch. He wanted to show her what she'd be missing since he probably still wouldn't agree to be her *date*.

Antika didn't even know him. Yet, she had dismissed him within five minutes of meeting, and Drevon could admit that his ego had taken a hit. Clearly, she hadn't realized he was *Drevon Ross*, one of the top twenty male models of all time.

A sensation Drevon couldn't quite identify prickled the back of his neck, and he rolled his shoulders before glancing up. That's when he saw her—a vision in red. Antika.

As she chatted with a woman who was standing near the opening to the dining area, he let his gaze rake over Antika's tall, shapely body, and he liked what he saw. She was wearing a real attention-getter. The red, one-shoulder jump suit tied at the waist emphasized her full breasts, and hugged every one of her luscious curves.

Hot damn.

She was prettier than he remembered. Now he was glad he'd accepted her request to have lunch. But all he could think about as the hostess led her into the large dining area was *why did a woman who looked like her need to hire a man?*

He also wondered what it would be like to kiss the red lipstick off her tempting lips.

The only way he'd find out is if he took this assignment. And right now, that was exactly what he planned to do.

* * *

As Antika followed the hostess across the dining room, she spotted Drevon. He was hard to miss, especially since he was wearing sunglasses indoors, which was ridiculous.

Then again, maybe it was a disguise.

As if reading her mind, he slipped off the glasses and rose to his full height. Her gaze traveled over him, noting the way he had one hand tucked into the front pocket of his jeans. Hell, someone could snap a picture of the guy right now. The man screamed fashion model with that pose alone. Head up and slightly tilted. Shoulders back. Arms and legs angled.

He looked seductive without even trying.

Drevon Ross was downright *gorgeous*.

He sure didn't look like he had the other day. Today he looked like a grown-ass, ruggedly handsome man who made her body tingle just by standing there.

No doubt every woman in the place had caught sight of him. He was hard to miss. Tall with wide shoulders that tapered to a narrow waist. The white untucked short-sleeved, buttoned-down shirt that he was wearing molded over his muscular body and hugged his thick biceps to perfection. And then there were his long legs that seemed to go on forever.

Yeah, he was hard to miss.

Calling Drevon yesterday had seemed like a good idea at the time, but what had she been thinking? He wasn't going to escort her anywhere. The man was so out of her league that it was almost laughable, and a twinge of self-consciousness crawled beneath her skin.

Was her outfit too much? Not dressy enough? Did it bring

too much attention to her hips? Was it camouflaging the little extra weight she carried around her stomach? She was definitely thicker than the women he was usually photographed with.

Antika slowed and ran one shaky hand down her side and over her hip while trying to take in a calming breath. Suddenly all her insecurities came crashing through her, and her heartbeat raced fast enough to leap out of her chest. Memories of how her ex-husband had swapped her out for a younger, thinner, and bubblier version slammed into her.

Don't go there. Don't go there. That inner voice of reason that helped her get over one bad breakup after another, screamed inside her mind.

Her gaze shot to Drevon. His eyebrows dipped slightly as he met her eyes, and she saw the concern swimming in his dark orbs. She forced her feet to keep moving, and as she reached the table he started pulling out her chair.

"Antika. It's good seeing you again," he said, and his voice was like a jolt to her senses. Deep. Melodic. Sultry. He leaned in, placed his hand at the small of her back. The heat from his hand, toasty enough to warm her skin, swished through her as he whispered near her ear, "Are you okay?"

Hell, no, I'm not okay, her brain screamed, but instead of getting sucked in by the anxiety swimming inside of her, she smiled at him. At least she hoped it looked like a smile, and then she nodded and eased into the seat.

"Yeah, ignore me. I kind of freaked out for a minute there," she said, and then groaned after saying more than she intended. "I talk too damn much," she mumbled under her breath, but apparently, she hadn't said it quietly enough because he chuckled.

He sat back in his seat and signaled for the server. Within

seconds, a perky brunette with beautiful green eyes was at their table.

"Hi, I see your guest has arrived." The woman smiled and turned to Antika. "Can I get you something to drink, maybe a glass of wine or a cocktail?"

"May I have a martini?" She considered ordering a shot of their strongest tequila to knock out the jitters, but thought better of it. She'd just nurse the martini in hopes that it would settle her down enough to string a few coherent sentences together.

Antika couldn't remember the last time she'd been this nervous around a man. It didn't help that the four women at the table next to them kept glancing at Drevon. She couldn't blame them. The man was oozing testosterone, and he didn't look like he even noticed the attention he was getting.

"Can you bring us a couple of shots of your best tequila?" he asked, and Antika's mouth dropped open, but she quickly closed it.

Was this guy a mind reader or something?

And if he was, that meant that he could read hers. Was that why he was smiling at her now?

"Are you psychic?" she blurted and after a beat, he burst out laughing.

"No," he said, still chuckling. "You looked nervous, and I thought a shot of tequila would help us—"

"I think I love you," she said without thinking. "I mean... um, I'm kidding." She leaned in and whispered. "For real, I'm kidding."

Now he was laughing harder, and Antika felt some of the tension ooze from her body. She couldn't help but laugh along with him at how she'd gotten herself all worked up. But it wasn't every day that you had lunch with a man this fine who had graced the covers of *People Magazine* and a host of other periodicals.

The moment seemed surreal, and she could barely wrap her brain around the fact that this was really happening. She was sitting next to a famous model with hopes of him being her plus-one for a few upcoming events.

After dating so many frogs, how was this suddenly her life?

The server brought their drinks and promised to return shortly to take their orders.

When Drevon lifted his shot glass, Antika did the same.

"To starting over," he said.

"To starting over," she echoed.

She slammed back her drink, then cringed as the harsh burn of liquor slid down the back of her throat and heated her whole body.

"Whew! That was strong," she choked out and coughed a little to clear her throat.

Drevon didn't look as if the drink affected him at all. He was skimming his menu. So she did the same while trying not to let it show that the shot almost knocked her out of her seat.

Antika decided what she wanted to eat just as the server returned. After placing her order, she stole glances at Drevon while he placed his. Soulful dark-amber eyes, smooth skin, and a full beard. A beard that appeared fuller than it had less than twenty-four hours ago. She loved a man with facial hair, and she wanted to run her hands over Drevon's to see if it was as soft as it looked.

And those lips. *Good Lord.* Full. Sultry. Kissable. Those were only a few adjectives that popped into her mind at the sight of them. What she wouldn't give for just a taste of...

Whoa! Stop!

What the hell?

How had her thoughts gotten that far out of hand?

She chastised herself as she looked anywhere but at him and her nerves started crackling. This was supposed to be a business meeting of sorts, but in this moment, if felt like so much more.

But right now, she needed to be cool and act like she was used to being around a hot guy.

When the server strolled away, he gave Antika his full attention.

"I owe you an apology," she said, trying not to fidget under his intense dark gaze. "I was way out of line yesterday, and I'm sorry for the way I behaved. I assure you that wasn't my norm. Sadly, to say, I wasn't at my best when we first met. Between nervousness about signing up for an escort service and just having a rough day, I unfortunately took my frustrations out on you. I hope you'll accept my apology."

Instead of responding, he searched her eyes. For what, she wasn't sure, but then a slow smile kicked up the right corner of his tempting mouth and she melted.

Whew! This man...

"Apology accepted," he said. "I'm curious, though. You're a very beautiful woman. Why did you need to sign up for At Your Service?"

Antika released a long sigh.

Oh, great. Start with the hard questions.

Chapter Six

Antika stopped herself from groaning, knowing her reason for hiring his services would make her look pitiful. Yet, she felt it was important to be as transparent as possible.

"I've been taking a break from dating, but I have a couple of events coming up this summer that I didn't want to attend alone."

"So, no male buddy you could call on? No friend with benefits that you'd prefer to go with?"

She shook her head. "Nope. It's just me. I've had my heart crushed one too many times. Now I'm embracing my singleness with no intentions of ever getting into another serious relationship."

Antika had been thinking about this a lot lately. She had once dreamed of getting married and having a family. When Patrick came into her life, she thought they could have it all. Happy marriage. Kids. A love of a lifetime.

Yet, their marriage had collapsed like a building made of playing cards. It took her awhile to bounce back from his betrayal and the hurt. Then, before she realized it, she ended up in one dead-end relationship after another.

No. Marriage and having a family were no longer for her.

Drevon was watching her in that way that he'd done earlier. It was as if he could see deep into her soul and knew her darkest secrets. Like he could tell that no matter how she tried to convince herself otherwise, the hurt—specifically from Patrick and Edward—was still lingering just below the surface.

His expression was a little unnerving, but on the other hand, she liked that he was listening to her. She didn't always get that with some of the men she'd dated, and it was kind of refreshing.

"All right, we have the jumbo lump crab cake and vegetables for you," the server said and set the plate down in front of Antika. "And for you, Mr. Ross, we have the grilled Atlantic salmon with asparagus instead of the squash. Can I get either of you anything else?"

Drevon glanced at Antika.

"No, this looks great," she said.

He turned to the server. "We're all good here. Thanks."

She flashed him a seductive smile and nodded.

"How does it feel to be recognized wherever you go?" Antika asked.

"You get used to it. Sometimes it's a benefit."

"Like when you can get the best seat in the restaurant?"

Drevon chuckled. "Exactly. In this case, it pays to be friends with the general manager," he whispered. "But there are times, like when I'm out with a pretty woman, that I wish people didn't recognize me. Overall, though, as long as I'm not approached while I'm eating, it's not much of a bother."

Antika nodded. She would never want to be famous enough that her life and privacy was no longer hers. She didn't hang out on social media much. Only enough to where she saw how invasive the public was when it came to a celebrity's personal life. They acted as if they had the right to know everything about them, especially during a crisis or if the celebrity had screwed up in some way.

For the next few minutes, small talk flowed easily between them, and Antika found herself relaxing even more. She could already tell that Drevon had a cool, calm, confident demeanor. She was used to being around arrogant, self-centered, high-strung men, and she found he was refreshing.

"Even though you agreed to meet me for lunch, I don't want to assume this...but are you still willing to be my date for some events that I have coming up over the next few weeks?"

"Yes," he said without hesitation, and giddiness bubbled inside of her, but she tried to look cool.

Surprisingly, she liked Drevon, and because she was wildly attracted to him, she'd have to make sure she reminded herself that this was a business deal. Nothing more.

"Oh, I almost forgot to ask you. Are you related to Mrs. Ross? I didn't catch it at first, but you two share a last name."

He grinned. "She's my aunt. My dad and her husband are brothers."

"That explains why you guys seemed so familiar with each other. There was a moment, when you were getting ready to leave the office, that I thought she was going to knock you upside your head."

He chuckled and wiped his mouth with a napkin. "She probably would've had you not been there. So thanks for that."

Antika smiled. "You're welcome, but I have to ask. You seem very successful. Why are you letting your aunt fix you up with women?"

"You've met my aunt," he said with humor in his tone. "She doesn't take no for an answer. Maybe one day I'll tell you how all of this happened. For now, I'll just say that you're the first woman that I've been fixed up with through the service. You'll also be the last. Like you, I'm not looking for anything long-term. Not even fake-dating the way we'll be doing."

"We're not actually dating, fake or otherwise," Antika said, her voice as low as his.

She told him about Tamera's birthday celebration, as well as the other events. They wouldn't be dating. He was just going to be her escort. As she explained again that she didn't want to go alone, there was no judgment on his face or in his words. She appreciated that.

But as she talked, she realized that there was one outing that she did need him to act as if they'd been together for a while. She needed him to pretend to be her man, and that's what she told him.

"My work event will be different than the others," she said and proceeded to tell him about the celebration her company was throwing for the managers. It was a black-tie event that would be held at one of the owner's mansions in Tuxedo Park, an affluent area of Buckhead, Georgia.

The event was a big deal, at least for Antika, because it was the first time that she'd played a major role in securing a multi-million-dollar contract. She was looking forward both to the bonus and the accolades that came with the recognition for her hard work.

She just wished that Edward wouldn't be there. Otherwise, it would be the perfect gift for a job well done.

"Congratulations," Drevon said and lifted his glass, and Antika did the same and clinked with his as he said, "Here's to many more successes."

As she sipped her martini, Antika studied Drevon, hating that she had prejudged him. So far, she liked him and could easily see them being friends. Then again, he'd already said that he wasn't doing this man for hire thing again. So that probably wasn't going to happen.

"Okay, so based on what you've said, I only need to wear my acting hat for your work event," Drevon said. "But for everything else, I'm basically your...what...plus one?"

"Exactly."

He nodded, looking at her in that intense way again. "So who is he?"

Antika frowned. "Who is who?"

"The man who you're trying to convince that you've moved on."

All she could do was stare at Drevon, wondering how he had put that together. Instead of denying it, she decided to come clean.

"His name is Edward, and like me, he's a district manager. Let's just say I shouldn't have ever dated him."

Not only shouldn't she have dated someone she worked so closely with, but he should've been her last choice. Antika hadn't realized it immediately, but it hadn't taken long to know that they weren't compatible. Yet, she didn't break things off with him.

For the next few minutes, she gave Drevon some insight into the relationship without sharing too much. She also told him more about her job and the company. Learning that he was also a wine connoisseur and collector, she hoped there would be a chance for her to see his collection.

The more they talked, the more they learned about each other. He had an older sister, while she grew up with three brothers. It was interesting to learn that he had started his modeling career while in college after an agent ran into him on campus. When the agent asked him if he had ever considered modeling, he had first thought she was kidding, but soon learned she'd been serious. Ten years later he was at the top of his career.

Recently, he had become a freelance model, no longer represented by an agency. He booked his own jobs.

"Isn't that hard?" Antika asked, wondering why someone would want to take on that responsibility.

"Not really. I've been modeling for so long now that I've made some great connections. Representing myself gives me more freedom to do what I want and when."

Antika's respect for him rose a bit more. She loved her job, but there were times when she wouldn't mind doing her own thing. But she wasn't a risk-taker, and she liked the idea of a steady income. If she went on her own, that might not be the case.

"I've heard that female models barely eat," Antika said between bites. "Is that the case for male models? Are you guys always counting calories or depriving yourselves of carbs and desserts?"

"Sometimes." Drevon grinned, and it felt as if someone opened the blinds and let the sunshine in.

Damn, this man was gorgeous.

What the hell had she been thinking the other day when she'd basically said that he wasn't her type? He was every woman's type.

Unfortunately, she could see herself falling for him—which was something she couldn't let happen. If her ex-husband and the men who came after him had the ability to hurt her, Drevon had the ability to break her beyond repair.

That was all the more reason to protect herself and keep the walls up around her heart.

"I've always been a healthy eater and enjoyed working out," Drevon explained. "So when I started my modeling career, I only had to make a few minor changes. But I am mindful of what I eat especially when I'm preparing for a big modeling shoot. Right now, I'm taking some time off to figure out a few things."

The nosy part of her wanted to ask what type of things he had to figure out, but that was none of her business. They were just getting to know each other so that when they were out together in public, they could at least look as if they'd spent time together.

Drevon wiped his mouth with the cloth napkin, set it on the table, then grasped her hand. An electric current of desire scurried up her arm and sent a bolt of awareness to every cell in her body.

He leaned in close, and his alluring scent surrounded her. "I have a feeling we're going to have a good time together," he whispered close to her ear. "I'm looking forward to being your plus-one."

Antika swallowed hard. With the way he was looking at her, and the feel of his hand around hers, she was looking forward to it...a little too much.

She wasn't sure how things were going to go between them, but she had no doubt that the next few weeks with him were going to be interesting.

Chapter Seven

Drevon inhaled deeply, his mouth watering at the scent of barbecue filling the kitchen. Though the sun had set, he had decided to do some grilling and had just finished.

He set the pan of burgers, chicken, and bratwurst on the counter. Now he had to finish up a couple of side dishes. He had just taken the baked beans out of the oven when his cell phone rang.

He moved to the other side of the kitchen and grabbed the device off the counter.

"Hello," he said and started back toward the stove.

"Dre, it's me. Don't hang up. I need to talk to..."

He disconnected the call and gripped the phone tight enough to break it as anger charged through his body. Blocking Kendall's number hadn't been enough. She'd been calling off and on for the last few months using a different phone.

Drevon didn't hate anyone—except his ex. She'd been the cause of the worst time in his life. As far as he was concerned, she could drop off a cliff and he wouldn't look over the edge after her.

He inhaled deeply, then released a slow breath while trying to clear his mind. He wasn't letting that witch ruin his evening.

When he finally got his breathing under control, the doorbell rang.

"Dang, they're here already?" he murmured, and glanced at the clock on the microwave, surprised at how the time had flown. He and the guys—his cousin Montez, and their best friend, John Edward Thomas (Jet)—were getting ready to have a late dinner and watch a couple of boxing matches on Pay Per View later.

As Drevon jogged down the stairs to the front door, he used his forearm to wipe sweat from his forehead. He'd been on his back deck for the past hour. One thing he hadn't missed by being away was Atlanta's summer temperature. It might've been June, but he couldn't remember the last time the temps reached the high nineties so early in the season.

He swung open the front door and grinned at the frown on his friend's face.

"What took you so long?" Jet barged into the townhouse carrying a case of beer, potato chips, and a duffel bag. "I hate all of these damn levels you have." He made his displeasure known by stomping up the stairs.

"You do realize you complain about my place every time you stop by. Yet, you keep coming back," Drevon countered. "Next time, stay your ass at home."

The stairs were one of the things that Drevon liked about the three-story townhouse located in Alpharetta, a suburb of Atlanta. The various levels made the twenty-two hundred square foot space seem even larger, and it offered room for him to spread out.

The lower level, where he usually entered his home from

the two-car garage, was where his guest room was located. The large space had an attached bathroom, giving anyone who stayed with him their own private sanctuary.

The kitchen, located on the second level, had a glassed-in corner wine cellar which made it one of his favorite spaces in the house. Also on that floor was a large deck, dining room, living room, and a powder room. His bedroom, which included a huge en suite, was on the third level, along with another guest room, bathroom, and his listening room that held his record collection.

Though he had a place in New York, it didn't compare to his townhouse. Atlanta was home. This was where his family lived; except for his sister, who was three years older. She and her husband, along with their two kids, lived in Los Angeles, but everyone else was in Georgia.

When Drevon reached the kitchen, Jet was loading the beers into the refrigerator. Clothed in a nice polo shirt and dress pants, with diamond studs glittering in his earlobe, he was dressier than usual when it came to them hanging out.

"Where you coming from?" Drevon asked as he stirred the baked beans before putting them back into the oven for a few more minutes.

Jet was a landscaper by trade and got many of his clients through At Your Service. He also dabbled in photography. He treated it like a hobby, but the guy could easily pursue a career in the industry. Drevon had introduced him to a few professional photographers, but Jet didn't seem ready to make the leap.

"I had to look at a couple of jobs before I came," Jet explained.

Drevon smirked. Considering how he was dressed, no doubt one of those jobs, if not all, was for a pretty lady. The guy had always been popular with the women and drew them to him like bees to honey. That hadn't changed over time. Six feet tall with tawny brown skin, full beard, and "good hair" that the girls used to go crazy over, they still gravitated to him.

"I'm so hungry. I don't know whether to grab something to eat now or change clothes first," Jet said as he speared a bratwurst and stuffed it into a hot dog bun.

Clearly, he had decided to eat first.

"Where's Montez?" Drevon asked.

"He should be here in a little while. He said he had to finish up some work stuff. At Your Service is thinking about updating their marketing campaign." Montez, the VP of marketing for the company, put in a lot of hours, but he always made time to hang out.

Jet mentioning Montez being at work had Drevon thinking about Antika. She had definitely left an impression on him earlier at lunch, and he was looking forward to seeing her again. Unfortunately, that wouldn't be until next Saturday at her friend's birthday party.

"These fights better be good tonight, because I could've gotten into something else. You know what I'm saying?" Jet asked with a smirk.

Drevon chuckled. He could imagine what his friend was saying, and it probably had something to do with women.

Jet and Montez were players and would probably never settle down. Actually, despite all of them being in their mid-thirties, none of them were ready to give up their bachelor cards.

Including Drevon.

Jet snapped his fingers. "That reminds me, I need to make a phone call." He pulled out his cell and headed to the living room.

While he did that, Drevon did something he'd been thinking about doing. He shot off a text to Antika.

Drevon: *This is Dre. I have questions.*

He smiled as he sent the text. He had considered asking her out for coffee tomorrow but decided against it. He'd wait until next Saturday to see her, but in the meantime, he'd inundate her with text messages, and maybe a phone call or two in an effort to get to know her better.

His phone pinged with a text message. Glancing at the screen, he read it, then started laughing.

Antika: *Sounds like a personal problem to me.* She added a laughing emoji.

Ahh, a sense of humor. Nice.

He noticed her humor a little during lunch, but for the most part, her nerves seemed to get the best of her. He had a feeling there was more to the former basketball player than what he saw earlier.

Drevon: *I see you have jokes. What's your favorite dessert?*

Antika: *Red velvet cake. Yours?*

Drevon: *Red velvet ice cream.*

Antika: *I'm not much of an ice cream person, but at least you have good taste in flavor. What's the weirdest thing in your closet?*

Drevon's smile dropped as he thought about the question. He didn't have anything weird, but now he was wondering what type of crap she had in her closet. *Maybe sex toys.* Nah, she seemed a little too vanilla for something like that.

Unable to think of anything else, he told her about the socks that his niece and nephew sent him with a picture of their faces on them. She responded back immediately.

Antika: *WRONG! That's not the weirdest thing in your closet. It's that hideous outfit you had on the first time we met. Give it to Goodwill. Better yet, burn it! Wouldn't want anyone else walking around in that matchy-matchy set. Burn it!*

Drevon's mouth dropped open, then he fell out laughing. He laughed so hard that Jet hurried into the kitchen.

"What the hell is wrong with you?" he asked. That only made Drevon laugh harder.

His friend rolled his eyes and went back to eating his brat.

Drevon struggled to stop laughing as he wiped the corners of his eyes with the heel of his hand. His interest in Antika skyrocketed. He loved a woman who could make him laugh, even if she was referring to a three-hundred-dollar designer outfit.

"It's just a crazy text that I received," Drevon explained while responding to her with five laughing emojis.

Antika: *You laugh, but I'm serious about that outfit. Burn it!*

Drevon: *I'm wearing it to the birthday party. I have more questions, but I'll text you a little later.*

Grinning, he dropped his cell phone into the front pocket of his jeans. When he glanced up, Jet was looking at him through narrowed eyes.

"Do you have a woman that you haven't told us about? Because you wouldn't be grinning that hard unless there was one on the other end of those text messages."

Before Drevon could respond, the doorbell rang.

"Saved by the bell," he said and hustled out of the kitchen.

Right now, he had no intentions of telling the guys about how Aunt Vi had roped him into going out with one of her clients. They would never let him hear the end of it.

Besides, he told them that he was taking a break from women after that fiasco with Kendall. Her antics were enough to make him want to give up on serious relationships forever.

I sound like Antika.

She hadn't given him a lot of details about her reasons for giving up on men, but hopefully he'd get a chance to show her that all guys weren't jerks. He just had to make sure he didn't fall for her cute ass.

Hours later, Drevon started taking snacks and drinks to the living room where his big-screen television hung over the fireplace. The third boxing match had started, but he and the guys were more interested in the following one—the main event.

"Damn, man. This is a lot of junk food. Do you have more people coming?" Montez asked, carrying the rest of the snacks that Drevon had left in the kitchen, including a fruit platter and trail mix.

"Nope. Just us."

Like Jet, Montez had arrived casually dressed. He casually mentioned that he had stopped for a drink with a woman before coming. *Figures.* His cousin was all about having a good time with the opposite sex, which was why he was meticulous about his appearance. He never missed his weekly barber shop appointment, keeping his hair cut short, and his mustache and goatee perfectly groomed.

Though it had been years, there were days Drevon still couldn't get over his cousin's physical transformation. While they were growing up, he used to be a skinny, geeky kid with low self-esteem who couldn't get a date even if he was the last guy on the planet.

Now he was built like a man who spent hours in the gym every day. He oozed confidence and a bit of arrogance, which made women flock to him.

Montez dropped down on the sofa. "There's enough here to feed a football team."

Drevon laughed. "I told y'all not to bring anything. Yet, you both showed up with snacks and drinks."

"We didn't know if you were going to have all of that healthy shit you always eat," Jet said as he munched on sunflower seeds. His friend was addicted to them. "Please tell me you're planning to indulge a little tonight."

"Why do you think I bought all of this crap?" Drevon said and dropped into his leather recliner. "Since I'm taking some time off from work, I'm planning to eat anything and everything I want."

"Ha! Tell it to someone who doesn't know you. You'll eat crazy tonight, but tomorrow, you'll be back to eating healthy and hitting the gym," Jet insisted, and he wasn't wrong.

"Oh, shit! I almost forgot. Guess what I heard today," Montez said excitedly, and sat forward. "Mom roped Dre into being an escort for one of her clients."

Drevon groaned. *Damn. I should've sent their asses home after dinner.*

Chapter Eight

J et's beer bottle stopped inches from his mouth as he eyed Drevon. "How the hell did Ms. Vi rope you into dating one of her clients? Wait. I thought there was a rule: no dating clients."

"You and I aren't supposed to," Montez explained, pouring some tortilla chips into a small bowl. "But technically, that doesn't include Dre because he doesn't work for the company. Still, he's family, and I'm pretty sure when the rule was created, he was included in it."

Drevon sighed for what seemed like the hundredth time during this conversation. "I'm not dating anyone. I only agreed to escort her to a few events." He needed to have a talk with his aunt. He thought their arrangement was confidential.

"And guess what else?" Montez said, seeming to be enjoying this news a little too much. Drevon wanted to slap some duct tape over his mouth to shut him up.

Jet started grinning without even knowing what was coming next. "What? No, wait. First, how does she look?"

Drevon rolled his eyes while Montez continued. "I peeked

at her profile photo and she's nice-looking. She kinda reminds me of Queen Latifah, but get this...the woman used to play for the Atlanta Dream."

"Get the hell out of here! She played in the WNBA? Seriously?" With wide eyes, Jet glanced at Drevon as if wanting confirmation, and Drevon nodded. "*Day-umm!* Why didn't Ms. Vi pick me? Dre works so damn much he barely plays b-ball these days."

"Dude, I told you we can play this week," Drevon defended, but Jet was right—it had been a while since they shot hoops.

"They probably have nothing in common. What a waste," Jet continued, looking disgusted. "I need to talk with Ms. Vi. Dre can't appreciate a woman who can hoop!"

"Man, *shut up*," Drevon snapped, knowing he was wasting his breath.

"We need to get her out on the court to see if she got any game," Jet kept talking as if Drevon hadn't said anything.

Little did his friend know, Antika probably wasn't interested in playing. She'd had a career-ending injury, and it sounded like she didn't hoop much anymore.

Besides that, though Drevon was feeling the woman, there wouldn't be any other dates—including playing basketball—outside of the contract's agreement.

"Jet, hold up. I didn't tell you the funny part," Montez said, and Drevon wondered what else he thought he knew. "This woman didn't want to go out with our boy. She asked Mom to find her someone else because Dre wasn't what she'd asked for." Montez howled with laughter as if he'd just said the funniest thing in the world.

"*Whaat?* That million-dollar face of his didn't have a woman swooning this time? Like he's just an ordinary guy?" Jet laughed so hard that Drevon feared his bag of sunflower seeds would end up on the hardwood floor.

"Y'all get on my damn nerves. Idiots," he mumbled.

He had to endure one joke after another, and he tried to ignore them, but it was hard not to laugh. He might not have any brothers, but with these two clowns in his life, he didn't need any.

"His charming ass will probably make the poor woman fall in love with him," Jet said.

Montez snorted. "Yeah, but considering Kendall announced to the world that he has commitment issues, things won't go far."

"True. She also said he had issues in the bedroom..."

Drevon gritted his teeth. He knew they were trying to be funny, but Kendall's name was still a trigger.

For the next few minutes, they kept the nonsense going, talking over each other, and he was about ready to knock them both upside the head.

"This sister can probably *dunk* on his ass and—"

"Drag him around the court by his earlobe, then—"

"Enough!" Drevon roared. "*Damn!* Grown-ass men acting like you're still in high school. Enough about me! What's going on with you guys?"

"I'm just screwing with you, man. Quit acting so sensitive," Jet cracked, chuckling as he dabbed at the corners of his eyes with the back of his hands. "You're an easy target. Besides, nothing's up with... Oh, wait. Remember that landscaping client I told you was my math and science tutor senior year of high school—Amaya Walker?"

"Yeah, I remember," Drevon said.

"She used to be super quiet, wicked smart, and extremely shy. It's been kind of wild getting to know her again after all this time. She's an amazing woman. A powerful record exec.

Has a banging, curvy body. Super confident. Knows exactly what she wants..."

Back then, Jet had been one of the popular kids and wouldn't normally kick it with someone as quiet as Amaya. He mentioned her sometimes after a tutoring session, but that was it.

"You do remember that there's no dating clients, right?" Montez asked and narrowed his eyes. "That means you *can't* ask her out."

"Dude, I know the rules," Jet said defensively.

Drevon grinned. "He might know the rules, but I have a feeling Aunt Vi will be going upside his big head with her laptop one day soon because he *broke* the rule. I can't wait to hear all about it."

"Whatever," Jet said dryly, never denying that he might try to get with Amaya. "Montez, since you all up in our business, what's up with you?"

After a long hesitation, Montez said, "I met someone. Sorta."

Except for the sounds coming through the television, silence fell between them. Montez rarely gave details about his conquests, so they could tell this mystery woman had left an impression on him.

"So what happened?" Drevon asked.

Montez shrugged. "Nothing. We hooked up at a hotel, and then she left the next morning."

"Did you get her name? Maybe you could find her."

"Her name is Desiree, but I'm not going to find her."

"Why not?" Jet demanded.

"Because she left without leaving any contact information. If she wanted to keep in touch, she wouldn't have done that. We had fun. It's over. I'm good."

Drevon shared a look with Jet, and they both shrugged.

No doubt there was more to this than his cousin was letting on. Whatever it was, Montez clearly wasn't ready to speak on it. At least not yet.

When the main event finally started, all eyes were on the television, but Drevon's mind drifted to Antika.

All of this talk about women had him wondering what she was up to. He eased his cell phone out of his pocket and shot off another text.

Drevon: *What's your favorite movie?*

Chapter Nine

Antika jerked awake, her arms and legs flailing until she heard breaking glass. Her gaze darted around, afraid that someone had thrown something through a window. Her condo was several stories up, but that wasn't impossible.

She wobbled to her feet, then moaned and grabbed her head, which was swimming from drinking too much wine.

That's also when she spotted the broken glass on the table in front of the sofa.

"Crap!" Her wine glass was laying on its side in pieces, and red liquid raced to the edge of the coffee table. "No! No! No!" she groaned, glancing around frantically for something to wipe up the mess.

There was no time to run to the kitchen for a towel. She snatched the gray throw blanket from the back of the sofa and reluctantly used it to mop up the wine seconds before it could drip onto the white rug beneath the table.

That was too close.

She huffed out a breath, balled up the throw and placed it

on the opposite end of the table before she fell back onto the sofa. She stared at the broken glass, soggy magazines, and the stain on the wood table.

"What a mess." But she was too tired to care. Her head hurt, her eyes were grainy, and her mouth felt as if it was loaded with cotton balls.

I drank too much...

After an exhausting week, she had looked forward to Saturday night to kick back and relax.

Antika startled when her phone chimed beside her on the sofa. Maybe that's what had originally jarred her out of a deep sleep. She had dozed off at some point while watching the show *Ridiculousness*, which was currently muted.

Lifting her cell, she squinted at the screen. *Drevon.*

"Oh great, now he texts me," she mumbled.

She had been enjoying their texting back and forth earlier in the night until he said he'd get back with her later.

Clearly, *later* meant different things to different people.

Like a high school girl waiting for the cute boy to call like he promised, Antika had waited up. Or at least she tried to. The last time she'd looked at the clock before dozing off, it had been a few minutes to eleven.

Now it was almost one o'clock in the morning. A little late for conversation, but that didn't stop her from reading the text.

Drevon: *What's your favorite movie?*

Seriously? He hadn't texted for hours, and that's what he wanted to know?

Antika: *Do you know what time it is?*

Drevon: *Yes. Now answer the question.*

Well, I guess I know something else about him. He's stubborn, texts people in the middle of the night, and apparently has a ton of questions.

Antika: Love & Basketball. *Yours?*

Drevon: Biker Boyz *or anything from the* Fast & Furious *franchise.*

Surprise. Surprise. He didn't come across as the *Fast & Furious* type. She expected him to say something like *Hamilton* or maybe *The Wiz*.

Antika: *I'm surprised you're awake. Why are you awake?*

Drevon: *Watching the fight with my cousin and best friend. I didn't think about how late it was. Sorry.*

Antika: *What's your biggest pet peeve?*

Drevon: *People who ask too many questions.*

Antika sputtered a laugh, glad to see that he had a sense of humor. She had figured as much earlier. Who knew getting to know someone via text messages could be so much fun? She texted several laughing emojis, and Drevon responded almost immediately.

Drevon: *Sorry, I couldn't resist.*

Drevon: *I have two pet peeves: People who lie, and I hate the silent treatment.*

Hmm...interesting. She sensed there was a story there. She'd been known to give the silent treatment a few times. Hell, she had mastered it toward the end of her marriage. Before she could respond, another text came through.

Drevon: *Your pet peeves?*

Antika: *People who chew with their mouth open.*

Actually, she had a ton of pet peeves, but figured she'd start with a lighter one. No sense in scaring him away before she had a chance to use his services.

The thought of having a famous model as her plus-one for Tamera's birthday party was still mind-boggling. Antika was looking forward to it and dreading it at the same time. She was a simple woman who didn't venture out much past her comfort zone, and spending time with someone like him was way out of her norm.

Drevon: *Note to self: don't chew with my mouth open at the party.* Then he added several laughing emojis.

Drevon: *That's it?*

Antika: *I also hate people who are mean just to be mean, and those who put down others.*

Seconds ticked by without a response, and she wondered if she'd shared too much. After being married to and dating men who were arrogant, narcissistic, and sometimes misogynistic, she had no tolerance for mean people.

She recalled when she first married Patrick. He was charming, nice looking, and he made her feel special...desired. But within a year, something had changed. She hadn't been able to pinpoint what, but he no longer cared about her feelings.

Going from being the center of his attention to barely being tolerated had cut deep. Her self-esteem had been shattered, and it wasn't until she got picked up by the WNBA did she start feeling like herself again.

Drevon: *Noted. Last question. What makes you happy?*

Damn. This just got deep.

Antika sighed. Her days were so busy with work, she wasn't sure what made her happy anymore. She never had time to think about it, and right now, her brain was too muddled to come up with a well-thought-out response.

So she said the first thing to come to mind.

Antika: *Cookies; any type of cookies and warm hugs. What about you?*

Again, seconds ticked by before he finally responded.

Drevon: *Right now? Talking to you. Looking forward to next Saturday. Have a good night.*

Wow. He's good. What a way to end a conversation.

With just a few words, he melted her heart and had her looking forward to seeing him again.

Antika already knew Tamera's birthday party would be a blast, but now that she was getting to know her plus-one better, she had a feeling it was going to be a night to remember.

Come on, Saturday...

Chapter Ten

This was probably a bad idea, but Drevon couldn't help himself. After hearing Antika's story at lunch Saturday, learning why she hired him, and texting back and forth with her during the week, he wanted to do something special for her.

He wanted to make her happy.

Was it crazy? Probably. Did he care? Nope. He could admit to being impulsive on occasion, and that didn't always turn out in his favor. At least this action would bring a smile to Antika's face.

Shaking his head, he chuckled. He barely knew the woman, but there was just something about her that drew him in. He could already tell that she was a sweetheart, and any woman who could make him laugh after the crap that Kendall put him through deserved a little kindness.

He parked his Range Rover in the parking garage connected to the building where she worked and climbed out. Grabbing the cookie bouquet from the back seat, he headed to her office. Sure, he could've had the treats delivered, but he wanted to see her. And if he was honest, he also hoped to run into the Edward guy she had told him about.

Drevon hated when men mistreated women, and Edward sounded like a real bastard. He knew for a fact that there were always two or three sides to a story, and this guy might have a different version than what Antika told him. But he'd bet money that her version was closer to the truth.

What he'd say or do to Edward was yet to be seen, but more than anything, he wanted the jerk to see him with Antika. They might as well get their farce of a relationship started and plant a few seeds before her company's big celebration in a few weeks.

When Drevon entered the building, a citrus scent permeated the air, and soft jazz flowed through hidden speakers. He was pleasantly surprised by the modern design—a contrast to the nondescript exterior. Exposed brick on some of the walls, painted concrete floors, and high-end pendant lights hanging from the ceiling gave the space a loft-like vibe. The large area reminded him of some wine cellars he'd seen.

He glanced to the back of the building where a catwalk was overhead, located above the elevator area. Several people were crossing it, and he assumed offices were on the upper levels.

"Hi, may I help you?" the young woman behind the customer service counter asked.

Drevon removed his sunglasses and smiled.

"Oh, my God...you're Drevon Ross," she said breathily, her mouth agape for a second too long before she hurried to close it and sat up straighter.

Drevon almost laughed when suddenly her professional demeanor was firmly back in place.

"Yes, I am. I'm here to see Antika Wilcox. Can you point me to her office?"

"Sure. Well, I can get you to her assistant, and she can help you from there."

Drevon nodded. "Thanks."

As per the woman's instructions, Drevon took the elevator up to the third floor. He strolled down a hallway, passing a few people who gave him head nods along the way. He didn't stop until he saw a woman standing near an open door, smiling.

"Mr. Ross, nice to meet you," she said and welcomed him into a glass-enclosed area where a desk and a few guest chairs took up the space. Beyond her was a hallway that he assumed led to offices.

"I'm Megan, Antika's assistant. Is she expecting you?"

"No, I wanted to surprise her. I hope that's okay."

Megan grinned and nodded. "That's cool. She just got out of a meeting but hasn't made it back to her office yet. She's probably in the staff lounge. Give me one second, and I'll show you."

She typed something into her cell phone, then stuffed it into the side pocket of the yellow dress she was wearing.

Drevon followed her down a hallway that intersected with another one. The place was larger than he originally thought. They turned left and strolled to the end, but slowed when they neared a closed door and heard raised voices—one being Antika's.

"Leaving so soon?" a man said from the other side of the door, a bite to his tone that Drevon didn't like.

"Yep, because I'd prefer to be anywhere you aren't," Antika said.

Her voice came through, and it sounded like she was moving around, her heels clicking on the tile floor but then stopped.

"Careful, Edward. We're at work, and I'm not above

reporting you to human resources for harassment." A chair scraped on the floor. "Now move out of my way."

Megan mumbled something under her breath that sounded like *I can't stand him.* That made Drevon wonder if there'd been other conversations like this at the office.

There was commotion in the hallway behind him, people whispering, but he didn't turn. Instead, he moved a little closer to the staff lounge, debating about pushing his way in.

"I just wanted to talk to you," Edward was saying.

"Why? I think we've said all we need to say to each other," Antika whisper-shouted. "I'd be totally fine with never talking to you again."

"I wanted to wish you luck with your new man," he said, then chuckled. "I'm sure whatever's going on between you two won't last long. I'll admit that you clean up nicely, but I'm sure he'll lose interest like I did."

Her assistant growled under her breath, sounding like Drevon felt, but then she must've remembered he was standing behind her.

"Um...maybe I should have you wait for Antika in her office," she said quietly, pointing behind him.

"Actually, this is fine." Drevon moved past the petite woman and walked into the staff lounge like he owned the place. All conversation stopped, and two sets of eyes turned to him.

Antika's eyes widened. "Drevon? What are you doing here?" she asked, her gaze bouncing from him to the basket that he was holding and back to his face again.

"He wanted to surprise you," Megan hurried to say. "Isn't this wonderful?"

Drevon was so busy eyeing the guy who was standing too close to Antika that he hadn't even realized that Megan had followed him into the room.

"Hey, baby," Drevon finally said, and stepped to Antika.

Holding the basket in one hand, he slipped his other around her waist. He pulled her closer and boldly placed a lingering kiss on her glossy lips. What he hadn't expected was the powerful, charged energy that shot through him at their connection, but he tried not to react.

He eased his mouth from hers just as she slowly opened her eyes, a dreamy look gleaming in her dark orbs.

"Hi," she said sweetly, and Drevon couldn't help but chuckle. The way she was looking up at him—as if he hung the sun and the moon—had him sticking his chest out. With just a smile and a greeting, she had managed to make him feel like a king.

"Hold up. Your new guy is Drevon Ross...the model?" the man that Drevon assumed to be Edward said.

"And you are?" Drevon asked with as much disgust in his tone as he could muster.

The guy had the nerve to grin and hurried around the table with his hand out. "I'm Edward. I'm Antika's..." he stopped abruptly, and lowered his hand when he realized Drevon had no intention of shaking it. "I'm one of the district managers here. Nice to meet you."

Instead of responding, Drevon turned his attention to Antika. "Did I interrupt something?"

"No, no. I'm glad you're here," she said quickly, then smiled and pointed to the bouquet of cookies. "Are those for me?" she asked.

"They are." He set the basket on the table closest to them. There were three round tables in the space, a small kitchenette, and a striped sofa at the far end of the room.

"I can't believe you brought that many cookies here," Antika said on a laugh.

"I know how much you like them and figured you'd want to share with some of your coworkers."

He had purchased the largest bouquet the bakery had, and it held thirty large cookies in different shapes and flavors. The happiness he saw on her face made him want to buy a damn cookie factory. Her beautiful smile lit up the room, and Drevon loved that he was the one who put it on her face.

To think that all it took was a visit from him and a ton of cookies to make her happy. He'd clearly been dating the wrong women. Normally, it would take an overseas vacation or at least some jewelry to impress the women in his past.

"You guys dig in," Antika said to the small crowd gathered near the door and grabbed small plates and napkins from a nearby cabinet.

Drevon hadn't seen the others arrive. They piled into the room, most dressed in business attire, while a few college-age students were more casually dressed. Everyone talked at once, and a couple of people asked to get a photo with him. He obliged and hoped that his presence there today would earn Antika some brownie points with her team and coworkers.

People grabbed a cookie, thanked Antika for the treat and then left, but a handful hung around chatting.

As he posed for a photo with two young ladies, he heard Edward talking and laughing. But then he heard him mutter in a hushed tone, "There's no way I'll believe that she's dating this guy."

Drevon stiffened and anger simmered below the surface. He didn't look up to see who Edward was talking to. Instead, he glanced at Antika. She glanced at him, but quickly turned away, not before he saw the hurt in her eyes. She must have heard her loser ex-boyfriend, and that only pissed Drevon off more.

He moved toward Edward. "What did you just say?" he asked, a lethal tone in his question.

How the hell was this guy a manager? He clearly lacked common sense if he had the audacity to say something like that to the guy standing next to him. Especially with Antika in earshot. Granted, he had whispered the words, but if Drevon and Antika heard him, other people did too.

Edward chuckled and waved him off. "Ah, man it's nothing. I'm over here talking trash."

"Yeah, well your trash-talking is about to get your ass—"

"Dre," Antika said, the word snapping through the air like a whip. She placed a hand on his chest, effectively quieting him.

The heat from her touch through his linen shirt was like some calming elixir, settling him down. Drevon's gaze met her eyes.

Ignore him, please, she mouthed, then gave him a shaky smile.

It was clear the asshole's words had bothered her, and Drevon couldn't let Edward get away with that shit. Antika was a very desirable woman, and she deserved to feel like one. He had to say or do something, and he needed to do it now to shut the jerk up once and for all.

Without overthinking his next move, Drevon reached for Antika's hand and held it within his.

"I hadn't planned to do this just yet," he said as he dropped down on one knee, "but there's something I've been wanting to ask you."

Chapter Eleven

Drevon stuck his hand into the front pocket of his pants and wrapped his fingers around his diamond pinky ring. He had put it there earlier before lotioning his hands.

What he was about to do might go down as being the stupidest thing he'd ever done, but he was going to do it anyway. He hated when guys bullied or belittled women, and he especially hated that the jerk's words had hurt Antika.

Down on one knee, Drevon gazed up at Antika. Her eyes were as round as dinner plates, and her chest heaved. But then she narrowed her eyes slightly as if to ask: *what the hell are you doing?*

He ignored the daggers she was now shooting at him and pulled the ring from his pocket. It was by no means a typical engagement ring, but it was a white gold band laden with more small diamonds than anyone in that room had ever seen.

Antika and a few others gasped when he held it up.

Her free hand hovered near her mouth. "Dre, what are you

doing?" she murmured, and it almost sounded like a warning, but he ignored that, too.

"Antika, from the moment you walked into my life, I knew you were different...special," he said, smiling as he recalled her telling his aunt that he wasn't what she'd requested. "You're one of the most beautiful, amazing women I've ever met. Add that to your kind heart and quick wit, and that makes you the woman I want to spend the rest of my life with. Will you make me the happiest man in the world and marry me?"

She stared at him as if he was a Martian dropped down on planet earth. She had every reason to think that he was crazy, but at least this would shut Edward up.

When she hesitated too long, Drevon grinned and tugged on her hand that he was still holding. "Come on, babe, don't leave me hanging here."

Considering this wasn't a part of their "fake relationship" plan, he wasn't sure what she'd say or what he wanted her to say.

Wait. That wasn't true. He wanted her to say *yes.* Otherwise, he was going to look like a damn fool.

And as if reading his mind, Antika said, "Yes."

She nodded and her grin matched his. "Yes, I'll marry you."

Cheers went up around the room, jarring Drevon, since he'd temporarily forgotten that they weren't alone. His attention was on Antika as he stood and cradled her gorgeous face between his hands.

Might as well get this awkward first engaged kiss out of the way.

His mouth covered hers, and within seconds, he got lost in the softness of her lips. The kiss was like soldering heat that melted metals together, and he couldn't pull away from her even if he wanted to.

And at that moment, he definitely didn't want to.

As his tongue swept into her mouth, she tasted as sweet as he assumed she would. He'd wanted to kiss her at lunch the other day, but thought making a move like that would scare her off. Now that he was getting the chance, warmth spread through his body and ignited a need that he hadn't felt in a while.

Drevon savored every stroke of her tongue, but if they didn't stop, they were going to give her coworkers more of a show than was probably allowed at her job.

He eased his mouth from hers, but their lips were still only inches apart. "Can you get away for lunch?" he asked.

"Yes! Yes, she can," Megan yelled, and Drevon laughed. "Antika, I'll reschedule any calls or meetings you have this afternoon. If there are any that I can't change, I'll call you."

Antika didn't respond, she was looking at Drevon as if trying to figure something out. She didn't snap out of her trance until those still in the room started congratulating her. But there was one person Drevon didn't see—Edward.

He must have snuck out at some point. Good.

Drevon returned his attention to Antika. Even with everyone hugging and loving on her, she still had that deer-caught-in-the-headlights look on her face. They needed to get going before she came to her senses and said something to discredit everything that he'd just set up.

"Let's go," he said and intertwined his fingers with hers and moved toward the door. "Megan, thanks for your help today."

She grinned and giddiness oozed from her. "Anytime!"

Though Antika was almost zombie-like, she'd managed to lead him to her office so that she could grab her purse. Drevon wanted to get them out of their as soon as possible, because he had a feeling that at any moment, she was going to curse his ass out.

* * *

"Have you lost your damn mind?" Antika screamed and pounded on the center console the moment they were both settled into Drevon's SUV. "What the hell was that back there? At no time did I say anything about hiring you to be my fiancé! What were you thinking?"

Antika couldn't stop shaking. She was angry enough to punch him. They couldn't be engaged. They didn't even know each other. She had hired someone to be her plus-one.

Not a damn fiancé.

Drevon pulled out of the parking space and started the trek out of the parking garage.

"Okay, first of all, calm down," he said, his deep voice still doing wicked things to her body despite her being pissed at him.

"I can't calm down," she snapped. "This is my life. This is not some reality show or movie. This is my *life*, and I'm pretty sure it just imploded. Oh, my God..."

She gripped the sides of her head, feeling a headache coming on as her mind replayed bits and pieces of the last thirty minutes.

"I can't believe you proposed. More than that, I can't believe I said yes! I vowed to never get married again, and—"

"Antika," Dreven said with authority and reached for her hand. "Sweetheart, calm down."

"You keep saying that, Drevon! Just because you say it doesn't mean it's something I can do. You—a celebrity—just asked me to marry you in front of several of my coworkers."

Granted, he wasn't some A-list actor, but still...

He was known well enough that if this sham of a proposal got out, people and the media would talk. Hell, they would hunt him down.

"Are you trying to be the topic of conversation on social media again?" she asked, the question rhetorical. "Are you trying to have people all up in your business like they were months ago?"

Antika had read on the internet about what happened between him and his ex-girlfriend, Kendall. It sounded like a nightmare. If the information was correct, he had even spent a night in jail after the cops responded to a domestic dispute between the two of them. Seeing the way some people on the internet—people who probably didn't know him—voiced their opinion was awful.

Drevon released her hand and huffed out a breath. "I didn't think that far ahead. I heard how that bastard Edward was talking to you before I entered the room. Then he had the audacity to talk shit while we were all standing there. Granted, he'd said what he said under his breath, but if you and I heard him, others did too. I didn't like it," he continued. "My first thought was to knock his stupid ass out, but I refrained...barely."

"You don't come across as the violent type."

"I'm not. I can't believe my reaction either, but that guy is a piece of work. I saw the look on your face, Antika." He split his attention between her and the road. "I saw how he hurt you with his words. I couldn't let him get away with that shit. So I reacted. I wanted to show him and everyone else in that room, that you are more than worthy. That you can get any man you want."

His voice grew deeper and louder, and Antika's heart squeezed. She could feel his conviction with each word. No man had ever defended her like that. Even if he'd done it with a fake proposal, it was still extremely sweet. She felt like she mattered to him.

"I appreciate what you did and why you did it, but you

risked a lot." She glanced out of the window while that knowledge swirled inside of her mind. "And where are we going."

He flashed that sexy grin that always ignited butterflies to take flight inside her stomach. "I'm starving. I figured I'd take us to get something to eat."

Now that she thought about it, she was hungry, too, but then her mind went back to the staff lounge.

"You kissed me," she said, and her cheeks burned as she recalled the soul-stirring kiss that had made her knees weak. She couldn't ever remember being kissed like that, not even when she was married. "Our fake relationship doesn't include intense lip-locking," she said. "I'm pretty sure on one of the At Your Service forms I completed, I said: *no kissing.*"

Drevon chuckled, and the tension inside of her and in the car eased.

"Nice try, sweetheart, but I read your information from front to back—twice. There was nothing about kissing or not kissing on any of the documents."

Antika smiled, knowing there hadn't been any rules like that on anything that she'd read when completing the profile.

At the moment, kissing was the least of their problems.

"Dre, what are we going to do? Getting engaged, for pretend or not, is serious business. How are we going to get out of this without one of us getting hurt in some way?"

We're so screwed.

Chapter Twelve

If it ever got out that she had paid someone to date her, or that Drevon had proposed marriage to protect her honor, Antika would look like a fool. On the other hand, if the public found out that Drevon was in a fake engagement of his own doing, they'd crucify him.

"And where did you even get a ring?" Antika asked and glanced at the jewelry on her left ring finger, then slid it off to study it. Small double stacked diamonds circled completely around the white-gold band, sparkling bright enough to make her squint.

"How many carats is this?" It was probably a tacky question, but curiosity got the best of her.

"Seven."

"Se—seven?" she sputtered.

He'd slid a seven-carat diamond ring on her finger without having security guarding her?

"Wait." She glanced at his right hand. "This is your pinky ring. I saw you fiddling with it at lunch the other day."

She noticed it because whenever she asked him a question

that he had to think about, he started twisting it around on his finger.

"It is. I had to improvise." He shrugged. "I figured it would do for now, even if it's a little big. But if we keep up this...this act, I'm going to have to get you a real engagement ring. I wear that one so often, if anyone who knows me sees it, they'll know that we're not engaged."

Antika shook her head. "That's because we're not!" she insisted. "Edward might be an asshole, but he wasn't wrong about me and you. No one's going to believe that you, the man who dates models and actresses, is going to hook up with someone like me. I'm just a district manager for a wine distributor. Not some...some famous person."

He pulled into a Chick-fil-A parking lot, and Antika released an unladylike snort. "You wear a seven-carat diamond ring and eat here?"

He shrugged. "What can I say? I like their chicken sandwiches and their nuggets."

Antika shook her head. "This is crazy. We can't pull off an engagement. I'm not that good of an actor."

He parked the car but kept it running, and then undid his seat belt before facing her.

"Let's get a few things straight. First, I'm just a man, Antika. Sure, I've had a little fame, but that doesn't make me better than you or anyone else.

"Second, we might be in a fake relationship, but I didn't lie when I proposed. From what I know of you so far, you're an amazing, beautiful woman, and you're funny as hell. I might've dated women in the industry, but mainly because that's who was around. Any man would be lucky to have you as his woman, and until further notice, I'm that lucky guy."

Antika didn't know what to say. At the rate this man was going, it would be way too easy to fall for him. Something she didn't want to do, but he seemed to always say and do the right thing. Yet, she already knew that if she wasn't careful, and if she didn't guard her heart, she'd be the one getting hurt.

"Thank you for saying that," she said.

"I meant every word."

Instead of them going into the restaurant, Drevon went through the drive-thru to place their order. Neither of them wanted to be around people at the moment, so they ended up eating in the car with the air conditioner blasting.

"Have you considered reporting Edward to your HR department? From the little I heard, when it was just the two of you in that room, he was out of line. Especially when he said, *I'm sure he'll lose interest like I did.* You even mentioned that he's body-shamed you before, and after meeting the guy, I'm sure some of that took place at work."

Antika didn't respond. She could agree that Edward had crossed the line one too many times when they tossed verbal jabs at each other.

"The asshole's condescending tone and the inappropriateness of what he was saying shouldn't be tolerated, especially in a work environment."

"I agree," Antika said. "And to answer your question, no, I haven't reported him."

"But you've thought about it," Drevon said.

"I have, but as soon as I consider it, I think about that we dated. In hindsight, it probably wasn't one of my best decisions." She shrugged. "Actually, it was a stupid thing to do when I knew we weren't compatible. He caught me at a weak moment in my life."

Drevon grunted. "Yeah, been there. I know exactly what that feels like."

"Unfortunately, while Edward has said his share of inappropriate things to me, I've done the same. Our verbal sparring has been filled with insensitive and unacceptable comments. So I'd feel like a hypocrite complaining about him when I haven't done much better. Besides, I hate the idea of reporting him. Edward might be a stupid jerk, but he's excellent at his job."

"I don't give a damn how good he is at his job. He can't go around talking to people any kind of way. If he's saying inappropriate things to you, he's probably saying it to other women."

Frustration stirred inside of Antika as she considered Drevon's words. She agreed with him, and she'd hate to find out that he was verbally abusive to any of the other women.

"You're right. I'll talk to him and point out that even if we don't like each other, we need to conduct ourselves professionally at work."

Silence fell between them as they ate their lunch. Eating in the car was normal for her, but Antika couldn't imagine Drevon doing it on the regular. She was also surprised that he ate fast food but kept that thought to herself.

His cell phone rang through the SUV's speakers. Instead of a name showing on the dashboard, a telephone number popped up. He didn't answer. Two minutes later, his phone rang again with the same number.

Antika glanced at him, his handsome profile tense. "If you need to answer that, I can plug my ears. Or make myself smaller and pretend I'm not here and give you some privacy."

Drevon chuckled. "You're funny, sometimes even without trying to be. There are moments, like now, where it feels like we've known each other longer than a few days."

Antika had to agree. It had been a long time since she felt this comfortable with a man.

His phone rang again. Same number.

"Or if you'd prefer, I can always step out of the vehicle to give you privacy," Antika said, wondering why she hadn't thought of that in the first place.

Drevon growled under his breath. "That's not necessary. I think it's Kendall, my ex," he said dryly and continued eating. "For whatever reason, she's been calling a lot lately."

"Why don't you just talk to her? See what she wants."

"I don't give a damn what she wants," he said, disgust dripping from each word. "She's the last person I want to talk to."

"Then why not block her number?"

"I did. She's either using a burner phone or has a different number. I'm not positive it's her, but I have a feeling it is."

Antika nodded. He had mentioned previously to her about how Kendall had been calling for the last few weeks. Even though he accused her of stalking and had threatened to get the cops involved, she was still calling. Or at least he thought she was, but he might never know for sure if it's her if he didn't answer the phone.

"If it was someone else, like a couple of potential investors I have calls into, they'd leave a message. It's her. I'd bet money on it." He finished off his sandwich and grabbed the peach milkshake that was sitting in the cupholder. "Want some?" he stretched the cup out to her.

"No, I'm good, but thanks," she said, as she finished off her fries.

"I just thought of something." Drevon wiped his mouth with a napkin and turned to face her. "This fake engagement might help us both."

Antika snorted, then quickly covered her mouth. "Sorry, but how can anything good come from a fake engagement? We've set up a lie and at some point, we'll have to come clean."

"Hear me out. If we move forward with this, you'll have a plus-one for the foreseeable future." He wiggled his eyebrows, and she laughed. "And I'll be able to get Kendall off my back without getting the cops or a court involved. It'll show her what I've told her more than once; that I've moved on. She'll see that I'm crazy in love with someone else who I plan to marry.

"Also, I have a couple of meetings with investors over the next few weeks. I know of one that I'd love for you to attend with me. It's in New York. The investor will be in town a few days with his wife, and he suggested that I meet them for dinner."

As he continued talking about the meetings and what he was expecting, the more excited he became about the possibilities. He was thinking that him being in a *loving* relationship might come across better to those who were considering investing in him and his movie project.

Antika could attend the meeting he had in New York. Not only because she loved the city, but also because she had a ton of vacation days that she needed to use before she lost them. She also liked the idea of helping him out since he was helping her by basically being her built-in date.

She mulled over all that he was saying, but there was one part that she couldn't wrap her brain around—Kendall. There was no way the woman would care or believe this charade. She'd assume that the relationship wasn't serious, or that it'll be over soon. Then she could go back to chasing after Drevon.

But all of that was beside the point. Antika wondered what would happen when Drevon was ready to get back to his life— the bachelor's life that he was living before she hired him.

What would happen to her? She was already falling for him. Could she maintain a platonic relationship with him until all of this played out?

Suddenly her chicken nuggets were like lead in her gut.

"If I agree to go along with the ridiculous idea, when this is all over, you have to agree that I'm the one who broke off the engagement. Otherwise, we need to end this now."

She should end it now for her own sanity, but the last thing she wanted to do was go back to work and tell everyone that there wasn't an engagement.

Drevon flashed his million-dollar smile, and she groaned inwardly.

Yep, she was screwed. There was no way she could be around this man for the foreseeable future and not develop feelings for him.

He stuck out his hand. "Deal."

Antika shook his hand. "Don't make me regret saying yes to you."

Chapter Thirteen

Drevon pulled his baseball cap low over his eyes, and stuffed his hands into his front pockets as he strolled up the street to a local downtown bar. After spending the afternoon with Antika, and laying out their engagement plan, he had called Jet and Montez to fill them in. He trusted them with his life and knew they wouldn't spread the news around, but they insisted on him meeting them for a drink.

Drevon rarely second-guessed his decisions, but he could admit to having second thoughts about his plans with Antika. He loved being around her. He also loved that he was able to knock her ex-boyfriend off his high horse, at least for a while. He even loved the idea of pretending to be engaged to her to throw Kendall off his scent. But the more he thought about this fake engagement, the more he regretted going about things this way.

He entered the crowded bar. Music blasting, glasses clinking, and people took up practically every square inch of the place. He pushed past a few who stood near the entrance, then glanced around.

"Hey, handsome." A petite woman who barely looked of legal age stood before him with a sweet smile on her face and sparkling hazel eyes gazing up at him. "Can I buy you a drink?"

He smirked. He wished he could say that was a new one, but some women had changed up their tactics. "Nah, sweetheart. I'm good."

Drevon moved away from her before she could say anything else. At first, he didn't see the guys, but then he spotted Montez waving from one of the back booths. Considering the crowd, they'd gotten lucky to snag a table.

As Drevon headed that way, he ordered a whiskey from a passing server and pointed to where he'd be sitting. When he reached the table, he slid in next to Montez.

"So I guess congratulations are in order, huh?" his cousin said dryly. "I can't believe you asked that woman to marry you... in front of witnesses. That's crazy, man. Even Jet hasn't done anything that idiotic."

Jet chuckled, not even embarrassed because Montez wasn't wrong. Their friend pushed the limits on almost everything, always keeping them entertained.

Jet took a long drag on his beer. "I'm starting to think that Kendall fucked with your brain, man, because you haven't been right in the head since you two broke up."

Drevon huffed out a breath. He knew his friend was kidding, but hell, Dre was starting to question his own sanity. He had not thought that proposal all the way through.

Montez and Jet tossed verbal jabs at him left and right, and all Drevon could do was grin and bear it until they wore themselves out. He expected them to have some laughs at his expense. The two kept harassing him brutally until the server brought his drink to the table.

"So am I ever going to meet my future cousin-in-law?" Montez asked, only half-kidding.

"And what are you guys going to tell your parents and everyone else? Oh and I'm sure Ms. Vi will straight up trip over the news since she is the one who threw you two together," Jet said on a laugh.

Drevon ran his hand over his beard as fifty million thoughts bombarded him at once.

Nope, he definitely hadn't thought everything through. It was a wonder that Antika hadn't kicked his ass or ran for the hills. He had screwed up everything, but he wasn't defeated. He was going to ride this situation out until the end.

He told the guys that he and Antika had gone back and forth on how much to share with their loved ones. Neither wanted to lie to their family. They decided they'd give Jet, Montez, and Tamera the truth, and they wouldn't say anything to the rest of the family unless it was absolutely necessary. There was a slight chance that the news wouldn't get out to the media.

Their biggest concern was their immediate family. If the news did get out, they'd tell them as little as possible, with the promise of filling them in soon. Drevon hoped it didn't get that far, especially knowing that his parents—especially his mother—would kill him for lying about the engagement and roping Antika into it.

"I don't know this for sure, but I think my mom asked you to go out with Antika because she was playing matchmaker," Montez admitted. "At the time, there wasn't a shortage of men or whatever nonsense she told you."

After spending time with Antika, Drevon had figured as much. His Aunt Vi had always been sneaky—in a good way. But she might not have been wrong about him and Antika. He could already tell why his aunt thought they'd be a good fit.

Antika was amazing. He liked everything about her. At least what he knew of her so far.

Besides that, she was a good distraction. Kendall had finally left him a voice message, complaining about how rude it was of him to not return her calls. She hadn't said anything else, but he was sure she wanted something. He just didn't know what...yet.

For the next hour, he hung out with his boys. Though his head was still spinning with concerns about him and Antika, he did feel a little more relaxed.

Montez looked at his watch. "Damn, I didn't know it was so late. I gotta get out of here. Let me out, Dre." He tapped Drevon's shoulder, trying to get him to slide out of the booth. "I have a date."

Drevon didn't budge. "A date, huh? With Desiree?"

"Yes, and I don't want to be late."

"Man, Montez, you and your girl must be getting serious," Jet said.

"She's not my girl. We're just hanging out and having a good time." He nudged Dre. "*Now*, will you move?"

"What if I don't want to?"

"Dre, just move your ass out the way before I move you." Montez shoved him, bringing back memories of when they horsed around as kids.

Drevon started laughing and stood. "Jet, I think there's more to this hanging out than he's letting on. Our boy has it bad for this woman. Oh, how the mighty have fallen."

"Well, at least I'm not engaged to a stranger." Montez chuckled as he strolled away from the table.

His parting words hit Drevon straight in the heart, and he dropped back into the booth with his hand on his chest. Before he could say anything, Jet started laughing.

"Man, you are so screwed. I have never messed up the way you did today."

"*No?*" Drevon said. "Because I have a feeling you're breaking one of At Your Service's rules—no dating a client." Jet opened his mouth to speak, but Drevon lifted his hand. "Save it. I'm pretty sure that was Amaya I saw you with the other day. You two looked like a lot more than friends. If you're going to sneak around, at least be more discreet about it."

For the next few minutes, they exchanged verbal jabs, talking and clowning about their individual situations. All was well until Jet glanced at his phone.

"Well, my friend. Time's up. Your big news is out into the world." Jet turned his phone around and on the screen was a picture of Drevon kissing his new fiancée in the staff lounge. The caption read: *She said yes!*

"Ahh, hell, and it begins. I need to warn Antika."

Chapter Fourteen

"How's it feel to be engaged for over twenty-four hours?" Tamera whispered, a wicked gleam in her eyes.

"Don't make me hurt you," Antika ground out between gritted teeth.

She wasn't in the best of moods since she hadn't slept well the night before.

One of her coworkers had posted a picture of Antika and Drevon on social media. The caption *She said yes!* would've been sweet, had the engagement been real. Despite the #weddingbells, #famousmodel, #kissing, and how Drevon was tagged in the post, so far, it didn't seem like the news had spread. But Dre said it was only a matter of time.

Finding out their business was out there in the world had been scary enough, but then this morning, Drevon had showed up on her doorstep...with a real engagement ring.

Antika had hyperventilated.

Her reaction hadn't been just about the ring, it was the whole situation that freaked her out. She knew this wasn't going to end well and had stayed up most of the night worrying. When she saw the ring, it triggered her, and she lost it. Her abnormal breathing after receiving the ring had scared Drevon so much that he had insisted on taking her to an emergency room.

Antika smiled at the memory. Thankfully she'd been able to calm herself down, but every time she looked at her hand, her heart rate increased.

She glanced at the gorgeous engagement ring on her finger. It was perfect. It was as if he knew her, knew what she'd liked. The two-carat halo diamond was set in white gold and had smaller diamonds that went around the band. It was delicate, understated, yet elegant. She hadn't been able to stop looking at it.

"I can't wait to meet my fake future brother-in-law," Tamera said, that mischievous glint still in her eyes. "He has amazing taste in jewelry, and the fact that he said that you can keep the ring when this is all over says a lot about him."

Antika couldn't argue with that but her chest ached at the reminder that this was temporary.

"Okay, I can see you starting to freak out." Tamera hugged her. "I won't say anything else about the engagement tonight, but can we talk about your outfit? I'm so proud of how you've been stepping out of your comfort zone, 'cause, *girrrl*, you are wearing the hell out of that dress!"

Antika grinned as she ran her hands down the sides of the white strapless dress that stopped above her knees and hugged her body like a second skin. She had never been skinny nor fat —somewhere in between—but she usually avoided skin-tight clothing as to not draw attention to herself. Except recently, she was embracing her womanly curves. She was getting a little bolder with her style, and not a moment too soon with Drevon temporarily in her life.

Despite the marriage proposal yesterday, he had made an exhausting workweek bearable with his funny text messages and even a couple of phone calls. But it was the huge bouquet of cookies that he personally delivered that had her practically falling in love with him. Not really, but almost.

Drevon had also included a note in the bouquet. Antika had stuck it in her pocket before letting her coworkers dive into the cookies. She had forgotten about it until she got home last night and read it. *Hope this makes you happy. A warm hug— coming Saturday.*

The whole setup had been the sweetest gesture that any man had ever done for her, and she would never forget it. Not only had he made her day, but he remembered that cookies made her happy.

On top of that, he had shut Edward up.

Yes, it was silly of her to care what her ex thought, but it felt great to see the arrogant jerk put in his place.

"You almost look as good as me, but I ain't mad, sis," Tamera said, bringing Antika back to the present. "We look *hawwwt!*" She lifted her hands up and snapped her fingers while doing a little dance.

Antika laughed, and she had to agree. They did look amazing. It was the night of Tamera's birthday party, and her friend was wearing a daring peach-colored outfit that crisscrossed over her breasts and tied behind her neck. The almost-sheer material hugged her midsection, and the long skirt had a deep split up each side that showed off her left and right leg with each step she took.

The garment was definitely a showstopper and left very little to the imagination. The color coincided with the gray, blue, and peach color scheme that she had for the decorations.

Tamera had rented a ballroom in a hotel located in the city of Dunwoody. She had been planning this birthday party for months, and by the looks of how beautifully the room was decorated, it was worthy of the event.

They were standing near one of the entrances, and Antika admired how the large ballroom had been transformed. Three long buffet tables were positioned in the center of the space and divided the room in half. The serving staff were currently bringing out food dishes and setting them inside the chafing pans. The scent of barbecue chicken and bacon-wrapped scallops wafted through the air. If the food tasted as good as it smelled, the guests were in for a treat.

Antika took in the round tables covered with light-gray tablecloths and how they were strategically placed. It was amazing how a simple room could come together so seamlessly. She never would've thought to put gray, blue, and the color peach together, but it worked. The hotel's event planner had outdone herself, and Antika especially liked the way yards of material draped from the ceiling, looking like waves. That, along with some twinkling lights overhead, gave the space a whimsical vibe.

"I just can't get over *your* transformation," Tamera said next to her. "With the way you're looking, you're going to have every man in here tonight swallowing their tongues. I don't know how your fiancé is going to handle the competition. Speaking of which, where's your man? I thought you guys were coming here together."

"First of all, he's not my man," Antika said, then glanced at the slim platinum watch on her wrist. It was an hour before the party kicked off, and she wasn't expecting him until then.

"We had planned to come together, but he lives in Alpharetta. He would've had to practically drive past here and go another fifteen miles to get to Atlantic Station," she said of where she lived. "I thought it would be easier for us to meet here."

"Makes sense, but before he gets here, promise me that you're going to try and have a good time and not overthink the situation."

"I promise."

Antika could admit to being anxious about seeing Drevon again, especially since they were pretending to be engaged. Still, she was looking forward to spending time with him. It was one thing to text and talk on the phone, but it was another to share the same space.

Drevon had asked her to travel with him to New York in two weeks. He had a couple of business meetings, and there was one where he'd need a date. They would be staying in his condo...together. She wanted to make sure they were both comfortable with one another before that trip and before her company's big celebration that was happening in a few weeks. But now that Edward thought that she and Drevon were engaged, it would be easier to tolerate her ex during the company's party.

Her heart rate kicked up thinking about all the time they'd have to pretend to be a couple. They would need all the practice they could get to pull off this farce. Well, at least she did. Drevon's acting skills would probably help get him through any situation.

For the next hour, she and Tamera took care of last-minute tasks and were finishing up when guests started arriving.

Antika's anxiety inched up. At any minute, she'd be face to face with Drevon. As if her thoughts conjured him up, he miraculously appeared in one of the doorways, and Antika's breath caught.

Wow.

Was it possible that he got better looking overnight? It still blew her mind that not only had she not recognized him the first day they met, but she had insisted that he was not what she had requested. The man was sex on a stick and no woman in her right mind would ever say that he wasn't her type.

Clearly, she hadn't been in her right mind.

While Drevon glanced around looking for her, she gobbled him up with her eyes. Casually dressed in a navy-blue linen button-down shirt with his sleeves rolled up to his elbows, his muscular forearms were on full display. A platinum watch and a thick silver chain-link bracelet graced his wrists, and he had on the pinky ring. The diamonds on it couldn't be missed. White, linen pants covered his long legs, but it was the white fedora on his head, tilted down just enough to give him a mysterious vibe, that had her salivating.

Her pulse amped, pounding loudly in her ears.

Tonight, he's mine, and I need to take full advantage.

The thought—bold and without shame—caught Antika off guard. But it was exactly how she was feeling. Question was, could her actions match her thoughts?

When their gazes collided, it was as if the earth stopped spinning and everything and everybody faded away. Left was the two of them staring at each other. Then Drevon flashed his soul-stirring smile, and Antika's knees went weak. She latched onto the back of a chair momentarily rocked by everything that was Drevon Ross.

"Okay, be cool," she murmured to herself, then stood with her shoulders back and her head held high as she glided across the room.

Despite his fedora, Antika could tell that a few people sitting at tables noticed him. Some were pointing. Some whipped out their phone and snapped a picture. That act reminded her of their precarious situation. She planned to dodge as many photos with him as possible, not wanting people to think that they were really an item.

That might be a little tricky, but it would keep her on her toes.

"You look absolutely stunning," he said by way of greeting, then leaned in and placed a lingering kiss on her cheek. Butterflies took flight in her stomach, and it took everything not to puddle to the floor.

"You look good, too," she said, unable to hold back the breathiness in her tone. "Thank you for coming."

Again, Drevon flashed her a sexy smile. "Yeah, as your fiancé, the love of your life, I'm obligated to be your plus-one."

That voice.

That deep, hypnotic voice.

It seeped into her soul, nipped at her nerves, then stirred something so deep inside of her that she had to stop herself from leaping into his arms. And the way his dark amber eyes, barely visible beneath the brim of his hat, glittered with lust, she almost fanned herself.

Goodness.

This man was what fantasies were made of. Everything about him sent her senses into overdrive and had her lady parts tingling with need. Then he moved closer, slipped his arm around her waist, and pulled her against his hard body. Antika's internal temperature skyrocketed, and she was fairly sure she moaned.

Remembering that their relationship was fake was going to be hard as hell.

"Where should I put the gift?" he asked.

So caught up in his nearness, it took Antika a minute to stop staring into his handsome face before she glanced down at the gift bag.

"I'll show you."

When she started to pull away, he maintained the gentle hold he had around her waist, causing her to look at him again.

He was staring down at her with adoration in his gaze. She still couldn't get used to the fact that she had to look up at him, even in her heels. It was wonderful. He made her feel dainty and feminine.

But what really caused heat to charge through her body was the way he was looking at her. When was the last time a man appraised her with so much adoration? When was the last time a man paid her compliments? Or when was the last time she'd felt desired?

And how sad was it that she was eating up all of it and yearning for more?

Drevon released her slightly and settled his hand at the small of her back. "Show me," he said.

Show me? She almost asked, but then remembered that she was supposed to be taking him to the gift table.

"Oh. Right this way," she said.

People smiled and greeted him as he passed them. He spoke to some and nodded at others, while keeping her close to his body as they strolled to the other side of the room. All the while, Antika felt like the luckiest woman at the party. So far, it didn't seem as if anyone knew about the engagement.

They stopped abruptly, almost slamming into a young woman, maybe college age, who leaped in front of them. Her raven hair flowed down her back, and her café au lait skin tone was flawless.

"Aren't you Drevon Ross?" she asked, getting a little too close for comfort.

"Yes," he said, his voice lacking the warmth that Antika had heard seconds ago. It was clear when he tightened his hold on her that he didn't want the woman's attention.

"Can I get a picture with you?" she asked boldly, getting in place next to him before he could respond.

Without thinking, Antika shifted her body until she was in

front of him, blocking the woman. "Baby, you told me that we wouldn't have to deal with this tonight," she said sweetly, and almost laughed when Drevon's left eyebrow quirked up comically.

He didn't miss a beat, though. His large hand glided up her back and pulled her against his chest. "You're right, I did," he said.

His gaze volleyed between her eyes and her lips, and Antika swallowed hard, afraid that he'd kiss her. They couldn't kiss. She might've wanted to, but they couldn't.

After that sensual kiss at her job, she'd told him no more kissing. She wasn't sure how realistic that was going to be, but she was going to try and resist. She already knew her tender heart wouldn't be able to handle it if he kept kissing her...if he loved on her lips the way he'd done yesterday.

As if sensing her anxiousness, he glanced over her shoulder at the woman who was standing there, looking at them with her mouth hanging open.

"Sorry, tonight is about my woman," Drevon said so casually that Antika almost believed him when she knew the real truth. "If you'll excuse us."

He eased them away from the young lady with such grace that Antika barely felt herself move.

"Sorry about that," he said, linking his hand with hers as they continued their trek to the gift table. "I often wear hats or glasses to try and move around this world without being recognized, but it doesn't always work. Thanks for the help back there."

Antika, feeling more relaxed than she'd felt all night, smiled up at him. "You're welcome. Glad I could assist. I don't know how you put up with women getting all up in your face and disrespecting your boundaries."

"Yeah, moments like that are a little off-putting. Some

women are bold and sometimes rude. Like they think they are entitled to a photo or conversation. The attention has gotten worse since that situation with Kendall despite her portraying me in a negative light."

"Yeah, Kendall made you sound like a real slimeball," Antika said, unable to keep the grin from her face.

Drevon laughed. "And you still agreed to marry me," he cracked.

Smiling, she waved him off. "Yeah, I'm always in support of the underdog." They both laughed. "But seriously, I know there are always two sides to every story."

"That's certainly the case in the situation with her. I'll tell you more about it one day," he said with a smile.

In that moment, Antika could almost imagine their arrangement turning into something permanent—a friendship or more. Anything was possible.

Then again, with a man of Drevon's caliber, what were the chances of him ever seeing her as anything more than a job...or a fake fiancée?

Chapter Fifteen

"There's Tamera, the birthday girl," Antika said, nodding toward where her best friend was talking to a group of people. "She's the one who told me about your aunt's company. Don't be surprised if she takes full credit for us being here together tonight." Antika laughed.

"So she's the person I need to thank for bringing you into my life. Yeah, I absolutely want to meet her."

He reached for Antika's hand and linked his fingers with hers. Every time he touched her, it was like a little zing shot through her body. She didn't want to read too much into the handholding, but her battered heart was doing a little jig inside her chest. She was going to have to be careful with him. She didn't know if he was just playing the role of being her date. Or if he was feeling what she felt—intense attraction.

They'd only been in each other's presence a few times, but the sexual tension vibing between them was impossible to ignore. But what if it was one-sided? What if once again her selection criteria had slipped out of whack? She'd been wrong about a man too many times, and she didn't trust her judgment.

Wait...

Why had she let her thoughts go this route? There was no future for them. If she didn't keep that in mind, she'd be the one with the broken heart. *Again.*

A huge smile spread across Tamera's face as they approached.

"Well, I have to say you're more handsome in person than you are on television and in magazines. I'm Tamera." She stuck out her hand to Drevon, and instead of just shaking it, he kissed the back of her fingers.

"Drevon Ross," he said, and released her. "It's a pleasure to meet you, and happy birthday."

Antika rolled her eyes at the way her friend was blushing and giggling like a schoolgirl.

"Thank you," Tamera gushed, her arm looping through his. "I'm glad you could make it to the party. Hopefully, you don't mind joining me at my table."

"As long as you don't mind if my date joins us," he said, easing out of Tamera's grasp and reaching for Antika's hand again.

Damn, he's good, Antika thought as his heated gaze washed over her as if they were devoted lovers.

Since arriving at the party, she'd had second thoughts about her dress, fearing that it was too revealing, too short, and too tight for her figure. But if the appreciative gaze he'd given her earlier, and the way he was looking at her now was any indication, Drevon liked what he saw. That made her like him even more, and it was going to be hard not to fall for his fine, charming ass.

"Of course," Tamera said grinning and looking as if she was going to leap out of her skin as her gaze volleyed from Antika to Drevon and back again. "But can I steal your woman for a second?"

"Sure. Would you like something to drink?" Drevon asked Antika.

She had already sampled the spiked punch when she arrived, but maybe a little of something else wouldn't hurt.

"Yes. White wine would be great. Thanks."

"Coming right up. I'll be back." He winked and strolled off.

She and Tamera stood in silence as they watched Drevon's tall frame saunter away. His long, confident strides and laid-back gait carried him to the bar in no time.

Dang, even his walk was sexy.

"Ooh wee!" Tamera whispered-shouted as she tugged on Antika's arm in excitement. "*Girrrl!* If I wasn't in love with Shawn, I would challenge you to a duel to win that man's attention!"

"Don't start. Remember, this is temporary. None of this is real," Antika said only loud enough for Tamera to hear. This was also her way of reminding herself of that fact.

"Whatever." Her friend waved her off. "That is one fine brother, and he is *totally* feeling you!" She squealed but slapped her hand over her mouth and pulled Antika farther away from the tables. "You better not mess this up. I mean it!"

Antika turned and grabbed Tamera by the shoulders. "Listen to me," she said, staring her friend in the eyes to make sure she was hearing her. "There is no me and Drevon. He's not mine."

"Yeah, but he could be," Tamera fired back, then cackled.

Antika huffed out a breath knowing that when Tamera got something in her head, she was like a dog with a bone. She was never going to let this go.

"I'm serious, Tam. Nothing is going to happen between me and Drevon."

A mischievous smile spread across Tamera's perfectly made-up face. "Yeah, you keep telling yourself that. I've seen how he's been looking at you. This might've started as an arrangement, but I have a feeling it's going to end up being so much more."

* * *

Drevon was in trouble.

Antika had gotten under his skin.

That wasn't supposed to happen.

Those were the thoughts floating through his mind as he held her close while they slow-danced to one song after another.

Tonight, when he first arrived at the party and spotted her, he had been speechless. There'd been an aura...an energy around her that practically knocked him out of his Cole Haan loafers. He'd been drawn to Antika like a magnet to metal, and he was defenseless to resist her.

Since then, and throughout dinner, he hadn't been able to stop looking at or touching her. That was a problem. This whole situation had gotten out of hand. He was only supposed to be doing a favor for his aunt. Not falling for this beautiful, sensual woman who beguiled him.

But Antika...*damn*. The woman had it going on. Pretty, smart, funny, and despite her being thirty-nine, there was an innocence about her that was endearing. And don't get him started on her body. God, she had a smoking hot body, and the seductive strapless dress and jewelry she was wearing had her looking like a Nubian goddess.

Yeah, he was a goner.

The song changed and Michael Jackson's "The Lady in My Life," flowed through the speakers. Without releasing Antika's hand, Drevon gently eased her back, lifted her arm over her head, and slowly spun her before pulling her back against his body.

She laughed and looped her free arm around his neck. "All right, Mr. Fred Astaire, I see you have moves."

Drevon held onto her other hand, pressing it to his chest as they swayed in sync to the beautiful melody. As she snuggled against him, he moved his mouth close to the side of her head and placed a gentle kiss against her ear.

"You smell amazing," he said, thinking that her enthralling scent of vanilla and some spice added to her seductiveness.

"Thank you. You do, too," she said, her breath warm against his neck, and an involuntary shiver slid up his spine.

This woman was affecting him mentally and physically. The smart thing to do would be to put a little space between their bodies. He couldn't. Not with how good she felt against him. She fit perfectly in his arms, like she was made for him.

Drevon tightened his hold around her waist and started singing along with the song. Some of the lyrics expressed how he was feeling. Like the part about how he could make her feel all right, and about how he'd make this a night they wouldn't forget.

Yeah. I'm a goner. And he wasn't mad about it. He wanted to know this woman better. She intrigued him.

Antika leaned her head back slightly and smiled at him. "You model, you act, and you can sing? Is there anything you can't do?" she asked, admiration in her tone. "You're full of surprises, and you're nothing like I expected."

Drevon heard her words, but he was a little distracted by her sexy lips that were inches from his mouth. Yesterday, before leaving her to go and meet up with the guys, he had promised Antika—no kissing her again. Why he made that promise was a mystery to him since he doubted he could keep it.

His gaze bounced between her eyes and her lips. All it

would take was for him to lower his head, or for her to lift slightly for their mouths to touch.

Was she thinking the same thing?

He wasn't sure, but he rarely deprived himself of what he wanted. And right now, he had to taste her again.

Before he could talk himself out of it, he kissed her. She didn't resist, and that was all the encouragement he needed to keep going. Their connection was like nothing he had ever experienced before, and he wanted the moment to last forever.

He remembered thinking yesterday how sweet she tasted. That hadn't been a fluke, and he was pretty sure it had nothing to do with the Moscato wine she'd drank earlier. He had a feeling that every part of Antika was sweet and gratifying, and he looked forward to tasting every inch of her.

As his tongue explored the inner recesses of her mouth, Drevon savored every moment. The woman, the kiss, and their nearness stirred something inside of him that had laid dormant for far too long.

But as that thought penetrated his mind, so did another one. They were in the middle of a dance floor. He might've been used to being in the public's eye, but he wasn't sure if Antika was ready for that—especially with the engagement hanging over their heads. And in the days of cell phone cameras, he never knew when a photo would show up on social media.

Drevon released a low groan, hating to end what he'd started, but knowing he needed to. With one last peck, he eased his mouth from hers.

As he stared down into her lovely face, Antika slowly opened her eyes. The dreaminess that he saw in them let him know that she'd wanted that as much as he did. She smiled and it was as if the sun was coming out after a thunderstorm.

Yeah, we're definitely doing that again.

Chapter Sixteen

After another slow song, the DJ picked up the pace and City Girls "Good Love," blared through the speakers.

"Yeah!" several people yelled, and folks came from every direction, swarming the dance floor.

Disappointed, Drevon reluctantly released Antika, and she took a step back. He could've held her all night long, and it still wouldn't have been enough. But when she started rocking her hips and shimmying to the beat, he got over himself.

Talk about surprises. The way she was shaking her fine ass, twirling, and gyrating, it was clear she liked the song. What was also clear—his date; no, his fiancée—had a little freak in her, and Drevon was here for it.

All of it.

Innocent, my ass. Gone was the innocent woman he thought he'd had pegged, and in her place was a spirited vixen. She was singing along with the lyrics, dipping and swerving her luscious body. But when she turned around, put her hands on her knees, and started twerking, Drevon almost lost his shit.

"Ahh, hell yeah!" he whooped and moved in behind her and started jamming right along with her.

For the next thirty minutes, they grooved with all the other party guests, and danced to one song after another. Drevon's mind was blown when a popular rap song blared through the speakers, and Antika started rapping the lyrics.

Damn, this woman was full of surprises!

At first, he thought that maybe that had just been a song she liked. It might've been, but when she rapped along with another song, and yet another one, he knew he was in love. Okay, maybe not really, but damn close.

He couldn't remember the last time he'd had this much fun, and to think, he almost didn't take on the assignment. It definitely would've been his loss.

"Okay. Okay. That's it for me," Antika finally said, panting as she dabbed at the perspiration on her forehead with the back of her hand. "That was fun, but I need some air."

Drevon agreed. With his fingers linked with hers, he guided her out of the nearest exit.

They weren't the only ones who'd had that idea. Groups of people stood in the wide, carpeted hallway talking and laughing, some with food and drinks in hand. Still, the area wasn't as crowded as it was in the ballroom. And the best part—no one seemed to notice them.

He glanced around until he spotted a slightly hidden alcove near a back exit.

"Finally, I have you to myself," he said when they reached the secluded area.

Antika turned to face him and placed her hands on his chest, and Drevon's arms automatically slid easily around her waist. They might've only known each other for a short time, but the energy pulsing between them was more powerful than anything he'd felt in a long time, if ever.

"You shocked the hell out of me with your dance moves," he said. "And that City Girl performance was worthy of a music video."

Antika laughed and gave him a sweet but shy smile. If her skin was lighter, he would've witnessed her blushing.

"And I think we have something else in common—rap music, my favorite. You knew every song."

That was a first. Most women he associated with were too prim and proper to dance the way Antika had, and they sure as hell wouldn't know the lyrics to the "The City Is Mine" by Jay-Z.

"You're right, I love rap music, and I love to dance," she admitted. "Once the beats start, I get lost in the song and my body seems to have a mind of its own." She shrugged and laughed.

Drevon moved closer, backing her further into the corner to shield them from others.

"We'll have to go dancing again sometime," he said, but then remembered that this was supposed to be a short-term situation. Instead of saying that, especially since he wanted more time with her, he pulled Antika to his side and placed a lingering kiss on her cheek. "Thanks for inviting me to the party."

"Thanks for coming," she said, smiling.

He loved the way he felt when he was with her. Powerful. Desired. Like he was a gift.

The thought might've seemed crazy, but the feeling was foreign, especially lately with all the crap he'd had to deal with in his personal life.

"I appreciate you being my plus-one."

He backed her to the wall and propped one of his hands on it near her head. With his other hand, he ran the back of his fingers down her soft cheek as he stared into her beautiful dark eyes.

"It was my pleasure, and I'm looking forward to all that we have planned over the next few weeks."

Her smile grew, and her whole face lit up. The need to kiss her again was overwhelming.

"Can I kiss you?" he asked, and she burst out laughing.

"Oh, so now you're asking?" she cracked, and he couldn't help the grin that slid across his face.

"Good point," he said seconds before his mouth crushed over hers. Pleasure radiated outward, and Drevon knew that a few kisses with her tonight would never be enough.

Antika wanted more.

She knew she shouldn't.

She knew she couldn't. Things were already complicated enough between them.

But kissing this man had her senses reeling, and that was clearly short-circuiting something inside her brain. She was ready to throw caution out the window and go for what she wanted tonight: Drevon. In her bed.

How crazy was that? But the heat that consumed her during that kiss on the dance floor was nothing compared to this one. Her desire bloomed into a roaring fire as this kiss rocked her to her core.

Her hands slid to his hard abs and worked their way up his torso. There wasn't a lick of fat anywhere her fingers touched, and she allowed them to continue exploring his upper body. The moment she reached his shoulders, she wrapped her arms around his neck and placed her hand at the back of his head. Pulling him closer, deepening their lip-lock.

Gawd!

She could admit that she had kissed her share of men, but none made her heart sing and her body tingle with need the way this man did.

Drevon moaned against her lips, or maybe that was her. Either way, they kissed each other with a hunger that promised of more things to come.

She wanted him. Wanted him more than she'd ever wanted a man, and...

"Ahem." Someone cleared their throat nearby, and Antika froze. She didn't take a breath until Drevon mumbled a curse.

As if on a spindle, their heads turned at the same time, and Antika's attention landed on a grinning Tamera.

Crap!

"Oh, don't stop on my account. Looks like things were just getting good. Carry on." She waved her hand between them and slowly backed away. "We can chat later, but Tika, if you decide to take that kiss somewhere more private, you have my blessings. Better yet, we can talk tomorrow. Late, *late* tomorrow."

Her friend hurried away, her laughter following behind her.

Antika dropped her head on Drevon's hard muscular chest and groaned.

What am I doing? This was not supposed to happen. None of this was supposed to happen. All she'd wanted was a date for a couple of events, and now she had a fiancé. It was almost laughable. Almost.

"I think Tamera might be on to something." Drevon leaned back slightly forcing Antika to lift her head. "Why don't we take this back to your place or mine? We can get more acquainted," he said, caressing her cheek with the back of his fingers the way he'd done moments ago. The gentle, rhythmic motion was driving her crazy, in a good way.

Her brain screamed—*No, we can't get better acquainted!* At least not physically, but every other part of her body was screaming—*Hell yeah. Let's do this!*

"Nothing will happen that you don't want to happen," he added, and Antika laughed.

"Yeah, that's what I'm afraid of."

"Come on. Let's get out of here."

Hand in hand, they left their hiding place. Antika wished they could just leave the building, but they had to return to the table for Drevon's hat and her purse.

Maybe by the time they got those items she would've talked some sense into herself.

Maybe.

Chapter Seventeen

They barely made it through the front door of Antika's condo before they were stripping each other out of their clothes. Drevon's shirt was tossed to the floor, and he had somehow unzipped her dress. It was now pooled around her ankles before Antika kicked it away.

Drevon backed her to a nearby wall, his mouth devouring hers like a hungry man who hadn't eaten in years. Their tongues tangled, teased, and they reveled in each other's taste as their hands were all over each other's body.

The ride back to her place had been twenty long minutes, and if it had been a minute longer, Antika would've begged him to pull over. That's how much she wanted him. That's how much she craved his hands and mouth on her body. That's how much she wanted to feel him buried deep inside of her.

He kissed her with an intensity that left no doubt that they wanted the same thing. And if the hardness of his body pressed against hers was any indication, they needed this.

"Damn, baby. Everything about you drives me crazy," he said against her lips, his voice rough with desire.

Same, she almost said, but when he slid his hand beneath the waistband of her panties, all thoughts fled her mind. Antika moaned, and her body sizzled from his touch while his fingers crept lower behind the lace. She opened her legs wider, longing for all that he planned to give her when he reached the entrance between her thighs.

More! Her brain screamed, and it was as if her lower body had a mind of its own, grinding against his hand, begging for more.

Her arms tightened around his neck as their kiss deepened. His touch was divine ecstasy, but it wasn't enough. She still wanted more. This wasn't like her. This greedy need to beg him to screw her until she screamed his name. She couldn't help what she wanted. Her body craved a release that would make her weak in the knees.

As if sensing her growing frustration, Drevon slipped a finger inside of her. Desire clawed through, pushing her toward a dizzying hunger that practically had her leaping out of her skin.

She ripped her mouth from his. *"More,"* she begged, pleased when he inserted another finger, and yet another, gliding them between her slick folds while his thumb teased her clit.

His digits massaged her inner walls, and a lust-filled moan escaped her at the pleasure he was stirring. And when his mouth touched her neck, Antika almost lost it. He kissed, licked, and nipped at her skin while maintaining a steady rhythm with his fingers.

"Oh, yes. Dre, yes," she panted, her breathing more labored as she rode his hand.

She bucked against him while he worked his digits in and out of her, going deeper with each thrust.

Antika knew it wouldn't take long for her release as her

hips rocked to the tempo that he had set with his fingers. While her passion grew, so did his speed, and her control slipped even more as she held onto him tighter.

"That's it, baby. Come for me," Drevon crooned.

A hysteria of delight built inside of her. It was the combination of that panty-melting voice, his fingers giving her a workout, and the delicious torture he was performing on her neck. Her body vibrated with liquid fire. Her thighs crushed his hand between her legs, and the passion simmering inside of her grew to a boil.

"Dre!" she screamed, unable to hold on as her release hurtled her to the point of no return.

Slamming her eyes closed, she clung to him like a lifeline while she shattered around his hand. Antika collapsed against Drevon, grateful that he was able to hold her up.

Ohmigod. Ohmigod. The word played on loop inside her head as her chest heaved and she struggled to catch her breath.

Minutes ticked by. When she finally lifted her head from his shoulder, she met his lust-filled gaze. He smiled and like a mechanical icepick, it chipped away at some of the wall she'd built around her heart.

His lips covered hers in a kiss that was so intimately sweet that Antika whimpered. Chest to chest, thigh to thigh with her arms around his neck, there was barely enough room between their bodies for air to pass through. She could feel how fast his heart was pounding. It was almost as fast as hers.

With his large hands cupping her ass, Drevon slowly broke the kiss and pulled his head back slightly. His dark amber gaze met hers, and her pulse amped. The passion swimming in his eyes was like a powerful wave, crashing against the seashore and knocking everything out of its way.

"I want you, but if you don't want this to happen, stop me now. Otherwise, where's your bedroom? Because there's no way I'm taking you fully up against a wall. At least not this time."

The low timbre of his magnificently deep voice had goosebumps racing up her arms. Everything about this man sent a welcome surge of excitement shooting through her body, and her heart was practically beating out of her chest.

He cupped her cheek and she leaned into the tenderness of his touch. "What's it going to be?"

"I want you, too," she said,

She blocked out the warning voice that was trying to penetrate her mind.

She wanted this.

No man had ever kissed her with so much passion, need, and intensity. No man, including her husband, had ever looked at her with so much desire radiating in his eyes. And no man had ever made her want to drop her panties the way Drevon did.

There was no turning back.

* * *

Drevon wasted no time kicking off his shoes, socks, and pants. He felt as if he was going to explode. His boxer briefs barely contained his dick that hung heavy between his thighs. And the sight of Antika pulling back the covers on the bed had him growing harder by the minute.

Then she turned to face him.

Damn. She was gorgeous. Some of her long tresses had fallen out of the updo hairstyle that she'd had earlier, only adding to her sexiness. She looked good in clothes, but watching her stand before him in white lace that covered her most intimate parts was like looking at an angel.

As his gaze went lower, his desire for her grew, and it took herculean strength not to toss her onto the bed and take her fast and hard.

He moved closer, his gaze greedily devouring every inch of her. He slid his arm loosely around her. "This body...this incredible sexy-ass body is mine tonight. And a belly-button piercing? You continue to surprise me," he said, fingering the diamond-studded curved barbell before bending slightly and swiping his tongue around it.

Antika gasped and her hands gripped his head as he slowly kissed his way up her scented body. He roamed over every dip and valley as he got acquainted with her luscious curves.

Everywhere he touched her, a frenzied sensation charged through his body. And the erotic sounds she was making during his exploration urged him on.

"Damn, woman. These..." he said, cupping her full breasts that were standing at attention and begging to be touched. He palmed them, then squeezed. Unable to resist, he pushed them together and swiped his tongue over her pert nipples.

Antika hissed. "Dre." The whispered word sounded like a plea as her hands gripped his head tighter which pulled him closer.

"I know, baby," he said, knowing exactly what she wanted and needed, because he wanted the same.

After another squeeze of her breasts, he released her, then finished getting undressed. When he looked up, Antika was sitting on the bed watching him.

"Wow," she said breathily, admiration in her tone as her gaze slowly traveled down his body and started back up again.

Drevon couldn't help but flash a cocky grin when her attention settled on his erection. "You like what you see?" he asked.

"Very much so," she said, and he almost came right then and there when she unconsciously licked her lips.

The gesture made his dick throb, and he hurried to grab his

wallet out of his pants pocket. He yanked out a condom and placed it on the nightstand before joining her on the bed. He wasn't sure who moved first, but before he realized it, they were in each other's arms again. Kissing. Touching. Moaning in pleasure.

Drevon kissed her with an intensity that stirred sensations inside of him that he hadn't felt in like forever. He moved from her mouth and brushed his lips across her cheek, her jaw, and then moved to that spot below her ear where he knew was sensitive. He nipped at her skin, and she responded the way he expected, twisting and squirming beneath him.

"Mm, you smell so good." All evening he had marveled at how enticing her scent was, and as she got more aroused, her scent grew more potent.

Drevon glided his hand down her side, marveling at how velvety soft her skin was to his touch. While his hands explored her incredible body, he moved his mouth over her shoulders, licking, and kissing his way down. With every touch of his lips and tongue, she shivered and the sensual sounds she was making amped the desire flowing through him.

He moved lower and cupped her gorgeous breasts again. He never knew he was a breast man until he saw her the other day in that red jumpsuit. Then again tonight in the white strapless dress. Each garment had highlighted her enticing figure, but specifically her full breasts.

Antika moaned and arched into him when he brushed his thumb over her perky nipples shortly before he tugged one into his mouth. He sucked her hard until she cried out.

"Dre! *Oh, my goodness.*" The way she dug her nails into his shoulders and clawed at his back, made him want to get inside of her.

He eased his mouth from hers. "Turn over and get on your

hands and knees," he said, and she stared at him for a heartbeat then snorted.

"Bossy, are we," she muttered, but did as he said, giving him an amazing view of her gorgeous ass. The Commodores' song, "Brick House" played inside his mind as he moved to the edge of the bed and snatched the condom from the nightstand.

As he sheathed himself, he glanced at her and almost lost his shit at what she did next. Gripping the headboard, Antika started twerking. Her hips rocked and her butt jiggled as she moved to whatever music was playing inside her head. Her moves took him back to the dance floor when she'd shocked the hell out of him.

"Babe, if you want this to last for longer than a few minutes, you can't be making that fine ass of yours clap like that."

She laughed and kept moving until he eased behind her and nudged her legs apart. It wasn't until the tip of his dick teased her entrance did she moan, and it sounded like music to his ears.

Drevon slid into her sweet heat, and her internal muscles gripped him like a fitted glove.

Oh, yeah. She was snug around him, but as he began moving inside of her, going a little deeper with each thrust, she adjusted to his size.

"That feels sooooo good," Antika murmured, her voice thick and sultry as she held onto the fabric-covered headboard and started moving with him.

Drevon gripped her hips tighter as he drove into her, his dick pulsing as he slid and out of her. She matched him stroke for stroke, and a hot tide of lust punched through him, stirring his desire as his pulse pounded loudly in his ears.

"Dre," she said on a moan, drawing out his name as her breathing increased. "I'm...I'm close."

With those words, her muscles gripped him so tightly, he

feared that he'd come before her. That never happened, and he sure as hell wasn't going to let it happen now.

"Dr—Dre!"

He didn't stop as she cried out his name. He could feel her getting closer to her release, and he wanted them to come together.

As she moved with him, chasing her orgasm, his thrusts grew more frantic. Adrenaline punched through his body and had him thumping into her like a madman.

"Drevon! Oh, my God, Dre!" She screamed his name over and over as an orgasm ripped through her, and within seconds he was right behind her.

His release slammed into him, and it was as if an electrical current arced through his body and propelled him over a cliff.

"*Shit*," he ground out before collapsing against her back. He cursed again, then struggled to lift himself up, knowing that he was probably too heavy.

Like she was doing, he held on to the headboard with one hand, and wrapped his other arm around her, and held her close.

"You okay?" he panted, and placed a kiss against her head.

Antika nodded, and when she released the headboard, they both crumbled to the mattress in a heap.

Laughing, he rolled on to his back and pulled her with him.

"Oh, man," she breathed and snuggled against his body. "That was intense."

Drevon agreed. He needed to get up and take care of the condom, but he couldn't move. So he laid there for a minute, marveling at how good they were together.

He'd had the first taste of what it was like to be with his fiancée, and he couldn't wait to experience her again.

Chapter Eighteen

Hours later, Antika laid staring at the white ceiling as her mind whirled at the pleasure that Drevon had brought her. Three times. Three orgasms in one night had to be a record, which is why it was going to be hard to tell him that they couldn't do it again.

It was already going to be hard to resist his sweet kisses while pretending they were engaged. There was no way they could add sex to the equation without her falling for him headfirst.

The bathroom door opened, and Drevon exited the same way he'd gone in there—gloriously naked.

This man's body was truly a work of art. He deserved whatever millions he was getting paid to model. Wide shoulders. Broad chest. Muscular pecks. Impressive biceps. There was no fat nowhere. The man was a god.

And when her gaze dropped lower to his semi-erection, she swallowed hard.

"We can't have sex again," Antika blurted, and he pulled

up short before he reached the bed. "I'm not even sure if I can handle kissing you while we're engaged," she continued.

He started moving again and climbed under the covers next to her. "Seriously? You kiss me senseless and used my body for your pleasure all night, and now you tell me we can't do it again?" he said, his lips quirking as if trying not to smile.

"I'm serious, Dre. We have to keep things platonic going forward. Remember, our engagement is temporary. After that, we go back to our old lives. No sense in making things harder for either of us when it's all over."

He didn't respond. Instead, he pulled her close and wrapped his arm around her. Reluctantly, she settled her head on his chest and snuggled against him.

Cuddling with him was a bad idea, but she couldn't help it. He was so warm and when he held her like this, she felt treasured...and protected. Though she shouldn't get used to it, she might as well enjoy it for the night.

They lay there in silence for the longest until she said, "Tell me what happened between you and Kendall. Why did you two break up."

"Damn, babe. Way to ruin the mood," he said it jokingly, but he eased his arm from around her and slid it behind his head.

Antika pulled the sheet securely over her breast and raised up on her elbow to stare down at him. "At least tell me what the final straw was that made you break things off with her."

"She wanted me to marry her, and I couldn't." He released a rough sigh. "I didn't love her. Hell, I didn't even like her, especially toward the end. We were only together a few months, and even during that time, we didn't see much of each other because of our work schedules.

"One night, when I was in New York, I stopped by her

apartment. I had to break things off, and I didn't want to do it over the phone."

"Such a gentleman," Antika said, and he chuckled.

"I told her that there was no future for us. That we weren't a good fit, and she lost it. Started cursing me out and throwing things around her apartment. The angrier she got, the louder she got and before I knew it, we were in a heated argument. One of her neighbors called the cops. When they showed up, she was still riled up, and told them that I had thrown a lamp at her."

Antika gasped. "Seriously?" She didn't know Drevon well, but she knew that he'd never do something like that.

"Yeah. They believed her and hauled my ass off to jail. I spent the night in county lockup. By the time I bailed out the next morning, she had spread lies about me on social media. So much so that I had my lawyer file a suit against her for defamation of character and anything else he could come up with."

"Did that work?"

"Yes, but the damage had been done. I was crucified on the internet until my publicist came up with a game plan to discredit her. This happened over eight months ago, and it wasn't until recently that we settled out of court."

"I'm sorry, Dre. I can't even imagine what that must have been like for you. I love that celebrities allow us to see inside their lives. Yet, I know it must be hell when negative stuff is leaked out and the public starts weighing in."

"Yeah, I wouldn't wish what I went through on anyone. Which is why I returned to Atlanta with every intention of laying low for a while." He looked at her pointedly and smiled.

Antika grinned. "Yeah, and then I came along and messed everything up."

Before he could respond, her cell phone ding, and Antika frowned. It was almost three o'clock in the morning. Way too late to receive a text message. It dinged several more times, and then Drevon's phone vibrated with several incoming text messages.

They both sat up and snatched their phones from the nightstand.

"Oh, no," Antika breathed, horrified by the photo that Tamera had found on social media.

It wasn't a bad picture; as a matter of fact, it was sexy.

But it was a picture of her and Drevon kissing on the dance floor.

More photos came through the text messages of them laughing and dancing at Tamera's party, looking like they were having a good time.

Her friend had also sent a couple of links to social media sites that led to posts. Each one had numerous hashtags attached to them, and though the photos hadn't gone viral, according to Tamera, there were a ton of comments.

Tamera: Hey sis! You're famous! BTW, I hope you're getting some good loving and not reading your text messages.

Drevon cursed from the other side of the bed, his fingers flying over the keyboard of his phone as he responded to text messages. Each time a new one came through, he'd curse again.

Several minutes ticked by before he glanced her way, a sympathetic expression on his face.

"I'm sorry, baby, but welcome to my life."

Chapter Nineteen

Antika felt like she and Drevon were really engaged. He'd done more for her in the short time they'd been together than her husband did the whole two years of their marriage. Granted, she and Patrick had practically been kids back then, but still. She now realized what a good man looked like.

After flying first-class, they'd landed in New York an hour ago. From the moment he picked her up from home, Drevon had been attentive to her every need. Now, they had just arrived at his condominium in midtown Manhattan.

"Here we are. Home sweet home," he said, pushing open the door for Antika to enter.

She strolled in, leaving him behind as he carried in their luggage. The first thing she noticed was the floor-to-ceiling windows and the ten-foot ceilings. Drevon owned a corner unit with a wraparound terrace, and even standing at the entrance, she could see tall buildings everywhere her gaze landed.

Antika moved further into the unit and glanced around the

ultra-modern space that was decorated in black, gray, and white with splashes of light blue. The kitchen might've been small, but it contained top-of-the-line appliances, white quartz countertops, and black and white flooring that looked like an art piece. Due to the open concept, the kitchen, tiny dining space, and living room could be seen from where she was standing inside the entrance.

"Oh, Dre, this is lovely."

"Thank you. I'm glad you like it," Drevon said, setting their luggage inside the master bedroom door.

With only one bedroom, they'd agreed that she would take the bed, and he'd sleep on the sofa that pulled out into a sleeper. Antika hated the idea of taking his bed, but there was no way they could share a bed and not have a repeat of last weekend.

"The place isn't large, but it serves its purpose," Drevon said.

He had explained that he used to be in New York more often when he was modeling full-time, and it made sense to have a place in the city. Now that he was freelancing, he moved around the world more, but he wasn't ready to give up his condo.

When Antika made it across the room to the wall of windows, she made a beeline to the terrace door. They were on the thirtieth floor, and as she stepped out onto the terrace, giddiness bubbled inside of her.

The traffic noise, people bustling about below, hurrying to get to their destinations, and the light breeze kissing her cheeks had her wishing she could stay there forever.

"Now, this is city living," she said to Drevon who stood beside her. Two comfortable-looking chairs and a small table were the only items out there. But it was the view that had her wishing she could afford to buy a place in the city.

"What do you think?" Drevon asked, his hands resting on the railing as he looked out over the city.

"I think I want to move here and live happily ever after."

He laughed, but she was serious. She had always loved the city's energy and being there with Dre was like the icing on top of a red velvet cake. If she ever got the opportunity to relocate to New York, she was going to go for it. It would be hard leaving her family and Tamera, but they could always visit.

"What do you want to do first?" Drevon asked. He moved behind her and pulled her against his body.

"Hmm, let me think."

Antika shamelessly loved when he held her close, even when they weren't putting on a show for others. Yes, she feared that she'd catch feelings for Drevon.

Actually, she was already crazy about him, but no way would she allow herself to fall for him. She couldn't afford to, but she had to constantly remind herself of that fact.

After their intimate night together, she had told him that it was a one-time thing. They had to keep their relationship platonic to make sure neither of them got in too deep.

It might've been too late for her, but she was keeping her feelings to herself. Drevon was an amazing man, and she loved being in his presence. But neither of them was looking for anything serious. At least that's what Antika told herself.

After her company's big celebration, she planned for them to go their separate ways—make a clean break. They'd break off their engagement and tell everyone that they'd decided to just be friends.

While that sounded like their best option, Drevon wasn't completely on board. He didn't want them to cut all ties. He insisted they should maintain their friendship, but Antika knew herself. Dre was one of those guys—she couldn't be friends with him. She would always want more.

Since they couldn't come to an agreement, Drevon made her promise to keep an open mind and not to do anything rash. She almost laughed in his face considering that was exactly what he'd done to get them into this situation.

Drevon gently shook her. "Well, what's it gonna be? What do you want to do first?"

"How about lunch? I also want to do some shopping while we're here. I need a dress for my work event."

They'd be in town for four days, and they agreed to go with the flow. Antika had never been good at that, but she was going to try. The only concrete plan they had was for dinner tomorrow night with the investor and his wife.

Drevon placed a kiss against the side of her head, and she smiled. Part of her wanted to remind him of the no-kissing rule, but she remembered that she'd vowed to go with the flow.

"Have you ever been on a carriage ride?" he asked, his breath warm against her ear.

"No, I haven't. You?"

"Nope, but I think it would be something fun to do with you," he said, and her heart flipped inside her chest.

"Dre..."

"Don't say no. Remember, we might be here for me to meet with the investor, but we're also on a mini-vacation. We're required to have a good time. So what do you say to the carriage ride? Wanna create a first for both of us?"

"Well, when you put it like that. Sure, let's do it, but after we get something to eat."

"Sounds good, but let's unpack and change into something more comfortable."

"Great idea."

* * *

While unpacking their bags, Drevon marveled at how domestic and natural it felt to have Antika in his space. He had emptied a draw for her and made room in his closet. It was weird being this comfortable with her considering they didn't know each other well. On the other hand, it seemed like they'd known each other forever.

They were just about to leave out the door when Drevon's cell phone rang. He glanced at the screen, not recognizing the number. His first thought was to let it go to voicemail, but then he reconsidered. He had several calls into people he wanted to see while in town. It could be one of them.

"Hold on a minute, babe. Let me get this," he said before answering the call. "Hello."

"How can you be engaged?" the person on the other end of the line screamed.

Drevon gripped the phone and gritted his teeth. *Kendall*.

"You told me that you didn't want to get married. You told me that was not a part of your life goals." She was still screaming at him, and Drevon started to hang up, but changed his mind.

"Kendall," he said, and glanced up just as Antika turned to look at him. "First of all, let's be clear. When I said that I'd never get married, I was talking about that I would never marry *you*. We weren't a good fit."

It was more than that, and she knew it. So he didn't bother rehashing something they had discussed more than once.

"No! Those are the lies you tell yourself. You know as well as I do that we're perfect for each other. And I saw a picture of your supposed fiancée. No way will I ever believe that you left me for her!"

"You can believe what you want, but she's the one I chose," he said, maintaining eye contact with Antika and meaning every word.

No, they weren't heading for holy matrimony, but he could see her in his life forever. Which was more than he could say for Kendall who was rude, self-centered, and manipulative. There would never be room in his life for someone like that.

"Goodbye, Kendall. Oh, and lose my damn number."

"Don't you dare hang up on me again!" she yelled, just as he clicked the disconnect button.

He blocked the number, then pocketed his phone before smiling at Antika. "Ready for some fun?"

She smiled at him, and that same heat that punched through his chest and made his heart beat faster whenever she looked at him was back.

Drevon wasn't ready to put a name to the emotion. Yet, one thing was getting hard to ignore—Antika was chipping away at the wall around his heart.

Chapter Twenty

They were only halfway into their long weekend, and Antika was enjoying every minute.

The carriage ride around Central Park, snuggled up with Drevon the day before, had been akin to living a fairytale. She'd only seen moments like that in movies and books, but to experience something so sweet and relaxing had her feeling like Cinderella. Then shopping in stores that she never would've ventured into, had taken her experience with her *fiancé* to new heights.

All she kept thinking yesterday was—*so this is how the other half lives.* This was also what it felt like to be in a loving relationship with a man who treasured you. Right now, it didn't matter that their charades had an end date. She was tucking away each experience into her memory bank to be pull out during those times when Drevon would no longer be in her life.

The thought made her a little sad, but at least she'd have the memories.

It was the night of the meeting with Drevon's potential investor, and they'd just stepped into the Michelin-starred

Italian restaurant. Antika inhaled the amazing aroma of fresh baked bread, fresh garlic, oregano, and other spices that made her mouth water. Though she was a little nervous about meeting this couple, she couldn't wait to sample the foods of the celebrity chef who owned the establishment.

"Right this way, Mr. Ross," the hostess, dressed in a sleek black dress and four-inch heels said, and led them through the restaurant.

Antika was glad that people barely spared them a glance, but that didn't settle her nerves. She tightened her hold on Drevon's hand. He was as cool as usual, and she didn't know how he did it. He was getting ready to meet with someone who could say yay or nay to supporting one of his lifelong dreams, and he didn't seem worried in the least bit.

"Is this okay?" the hostess asked, referring to the table located in a secluded area of the restaurant and perfect for talking business.

"This is perfect," Drevon said, and pulled the chair out for Antika.

"Wonderful. Your server, Monica, will be with you shortly."

"Thank you," they said in unison.

Drevon unbuttoned his suit jacket before claiming the seat next to her. They both were facing the entrance and would be able to see the other two people in their party when they arrive.

"How do you..." Antika started, but stopped when the server arrived at the table and took their drink orders.

Drevon rested his arm on the back of her chair and spoke after the server left the table. "What were you going to say?"

God, when he was this close to her, she could barely think straight. His fresh scent, his gorgeous face, his powerful presence, they all did wicked things to her peace of mind.

"I was going to ask how you feel and if you were nervous.

But considering you're not shivering next to me, I think that answers my question."

He flashed her a confident grin.

"I'm good. I've been working on this project for a while, and I've talked to so many people about it already. I have my speech down pat, and I already know this guy is interested in learning more about the project."

Drevon had told her a little about the action flick. The screenplay was done, and he had identified a film director for the project. He even shared with her who his dream cast would be. The movie idea sounded amazing, and Antika had no doubt that whatever Drevon set out to do would be successful.

She was so proud of him. Listening to him explain where he was in the whole process, and how close he was to seeing his dream come to fruition, made Antika made her want this for him. She also loved that he was comfortable enough and trusted her enough to share details about the project.

"They're here," he whispered, and they both stood when an older Black couple headed in their direction.

As they approached, the man's wife gave Antika a warm smile, which she returned, and she immediately felt comfortable.

"Mr. & Mrs. Hardison, great seeing you again," Drevon said and shook the man's hand and kissed the woman on the cheek.

"We're well past formalities. I told you to call us by our first names. I'm Graham, and this is my wife Janita."

Drevon nodded and smiled at the couple. "Graham and Janita it is—and this is Antika."

"Your fiancée. It's a pleasure to meet you, young lady," Graham said.

His wife squeezed Antika's hand and gave her another warm smile. "Congratulations on your engagement."

She and Drevon thanked the couple before they all took their seats.

Graham signaled for the server. "We'll have to order a bottle of champagne to celebrate."

Guilt sliced through Antika. Hearing the man refer to her as Drevon's fiancée was like taking a punch to the gut. She hated lying to people, but now that they'd started this charade, they had to keep it going. At least for now.

She was not looking forward to when they'd have to "break up."

* * *

Watching Antika chat with Janita made Drevon's respect for her grow higher. She knew how important this meeting was to him and had gone beyond the call of duty to befriend Graham's wife. He had already thought she was incredible, but seeing how well versed she was on almost every subject made him proud to be in her presence.

They were also a good team. He had told her enough about his project to the point that she was able to speak on it. He'd been even more impressed when Janita asked Antika what she thought about the project. She'd been able to articulate her thoughts, her concerns, and when she told the couple that she supported him one hundred percent, Drevon had been about ready to marry her on the spot.

She's your fake fiancée. This is not real, that irritating voice in the back of his mind screamed.

Still, even knowing that their relationship wasn't real didn't stop him from imagining what it would be like to have her by his side forever.

At the end of dinner, instead of leaving with Graham and Janita, Drevon and Antika hung out at the bar for a nightcap.

They shared their thoughts about how they thought the meeting went, and if there was anything he should include in future pitches to potential investors.

They had just finished their drinks when Drevon glanced toward the entrance.

Kendall and two other women stood near the hostess stand.

"Ahh, hell," he grumbled.

Kendall lived in Manhattan, but of all the restaurants in the city, why'd she have to choose that one? He already knew that she hadn't tracked him there since she had no way of doing that. His location setting on his phone was turned off, and only a handful of people knew he was in the city.

Antika's gaze whipped to him. "What's wrong?"

He leaned close to her ear as he stood. "Kendall is here."

There were quite a few people near the entrance, and she was deep in conversation with the women she walked in with.

"She hasn't seen us," Drevon said. "Maybe we can ease out of here before she does."

"Good idea."

Antika stook and Drevon folded her hand within his and led her toward the exit, but not before Kendall glanced their way.

Shit. Here we go.

At least they were close to the door and outside of earshot of those eating dinner.

"I know you're not trying to leave without saying hello," Kendall said when she approached, a sickishly sweet smile spread across her dark red lips. She lifted her face up to kiss him, but Drevon leaned back, causing her to kiss air.

"Don't even think about it. You lost that privilege a long time ago," he said, unable to keep the rage out of his tone.

Hurt flashed in her eyes but disappeared just as quickly.

"So, are you going to introduce me to your date?" she asked, looking at Antika as if she was shit on the bottom of her over-priced shoes.

"I hadn't planned to introduce you to my *fiancée*. As a matter of fact, we were just leaving.' He steered Antika toward the door where others were entering, but Kendall blocked their path.

"Oh, I see how it is. You're embarrassed by her, and don't want anyone to know you're slumming. I guess you have to settle for less when you've already had the best."

"*Dre*," Antika said in mock exasperation as she stared up at him with her hands on his chest. He recognized the mischief in her eyes and wondered what she'd say. "I don't need to meet any more of your groupies tonight. Can we go?"

Kendall gasped. "Excuse you. Do you *know* who I am?" she said indignantly, and Drevon couldn't help but laugh.

When he glanced at Antika, he didn't miss the smile flirting around her pretty lips. She was probably remembering what he was recalling—the day they first met. He'd said the same thing to her when she told his aunt that he wasn't what she requested.

That seemed like a lifetime ago but was only a few weeks, he thought as he grabbed her hand and kissed the back of it.

"Heffa, don't act like you don't know me," Kendall said, moving a little closer, but Drevon blocked her, making sure he stayed between her and Antika. "Don't worry, I ain't gon' do nothing to your chubby girlfriend."

"Be careful, Kendall," Drevon warned, his voice an octave lower.

"I just want to make sure she knows that I had you first." She looked around Drevon to see Antika. "You should be thanking me. You're probably benefiting from everything I taught him in the bedroom. So you're welcome."

What did he ever see in this witch?

"Jealousy is not a good look on you, Kendall. Now move out the way."

"Not until you and I talk. I've been calling you."

She sighed loudly and put a little space between them and flashing him one of her smiles that she used to use to get stuff out of him. He already knew he wasn't going to like whatever she had to say.

"I wanted to congratulate you. I heard that you're working on producing a movie. That's incredible. I hope you consider me for one of the roles. It doesn't have to be the lead, but I'm sure I'd nail it."

Drevon stared at her, assuming she was joking. When he realized she wasn't, he laughed in her face.

He inched toward her, but Antika held tight to his hand, probably trying to keep him from doing something stupid, like strangle his ex. He squeezed her hand back, hoping to reassure her that he had himself under control.

Leaning in, he said to Kendall, "You insult my fiancée, and you think I'm going to offer you a part in my movie? You're even more delusional than usual. You will *never* be a part of any of my projects. Not only that. If someone in the industry contacts me about you for any potential roles, I plan to tell them the truth. Find someone else, because Kendall Monroe is not worth the stress."

She reared back and gasped. "How dare you! If you even think about spreading lies about me, I'll—"

"See, that's just it, Kendall, they won't be lies. Now, I suggest you stay the hell away from me and lose my damn number or else."

He turned from her and gripped Antika's hand tighter. "Let's go, baby."

Chapter Twenty-One

The moment they stepped outside, Antika exhaled the breath she hadn't realized she was holding. She didn't like drama. She tried to keep it out of her life as best she could and being around Kendall reminded her why. It made people look like fools.

The woman had issues—and the sad part was that she probably didn't even realize it.

Then again, maybe she was trying to get into character for a reality show. One of those where people were always at each other's throats, tearing down one another, or physically fighting. If that was the case, she was nailing the role, because her behavior in that restaurant was deplorable.

How Drevon ended up with someone like Kendall was a mystery. They didn't fit.

Antika knew in many relationships, opposites attract, but those two? Nah, there was no way their relationship would've ever lasted.

Drevon was kind, generous, and didn't hesitate to step up to help someone in need, while Kendall came across as self-absorbed, inconsiderate, and dumb.

The fact that she was acting like a jerk in public—not caring that some of her fans might see or hear her—said a lot about her. She lacked common sense, and it was clear that the two women with her weren't really her friends. Otherwise, they would've tried to stop her from making a fool of herself.

But the kicker was when she asked Drevon for a role in his movie? Who does that? Especially after insulting him and his woman.

"So that was Kendall, huh?" Antika finally said to Drevon as he hailed a cab.

He snorted. "Yeah, unfortunately. Sorry for the crap she said and the way she acted. I wish I could say that wasn't her norm."

"No need to apologize. At least I see why your aunt was anxious to get you a date with a *real* woman." She wiggled her eyebrows up and down the way he often did to get her to laugh.

Drevon stared at her for a moment, then threw back his head and laughed. People walking by looked at them in amusement, and he didn't pull himself together until a taxi swerved out of traffic and stopped on a dime in front of them.

She loved making him laugh because he laughed with his whole body, and it stirred something powerful inside of her. Except for running into Kendall, this had been a fun night.

Actually, the entire weekend was turning into one of the best she'd had in a long time. She couldn't remember feeling so happy and relaxed, and it had everything to do with Drevon. She loved pretending to be his woman, even though she knew it was temporary.

Still grinning, Drevon wrapped his arm around her neck, pulled her close, and placed a tender kiss against her temple. "God, you crack me up. That's why I lo..." he stopped abruptly and jumped back as if someone had burned him. "I mean I—I..." he started again, then cursed under his breath.

In the weeks that they'd been spending together, she had never seen him less than cool, calm, and collected. Until now. Now, his anxiousness was palpable, and it was clear he didn't know how to handle what he almost said.

"You getting in the car, lady, or what?" the cabby yelled out the window. His accent was heavy with attitude punctuating each word. "I ain't got all night."

"Yes, we're getting in," Antika said quickly, nudging Drevon. "Right? We're ready to leave?"

"Uh, yeah. Yeah." He hurried and opened the back door for her, and she slid in. When he climbed in after her, he gave the driver the address.

The silence between them was thick on the ride back to his condo, and Antika wanted to say something, but wasn't sure what to say.

She wanted to let him off the hook somehow, tell him that she knew he didn't mean anything by what almost left his mouth, but she didn't want to. She had a feeling that they were experiencing similar emotions in this sham of an engagement.

"About what I almost said," Drevon started, but Antika stopped him by putting a finger to her lips and nodding toward the driver.

"Let's talk when we get home," she said, then caught herself. "Umm, I mean your home."

He nodded and reached for her hand. She never would've pegged him as a hand holder, but he took every opportunity to hold hers.

To be honest, he touched her all the time, and she liked it.

All of it...and that was a problem.

There was an unexplainable chemistry that lurked between them. One that she had never experienced before, making this new territory for her. Clearly, they both felt it, and no matter how Antika tried to deny the strong feelings, she couldn't. Their attraction was indisputable.

Thirty minutes later, they strolled into his condo. She kicked off her heels, glad to give her achy feet a reprieve and headed to the bedroom. Drevon was right behind her.

"I'm sorry," he said quietly from the doorway, and she turned to look at him, surprised that he had already discarded his suit jacket.

"For what?" she asked, dropping down on the bed and honestly not knowing why he felt a need to apologize.

"For shutting down the way I did. For not completing the statement that I started before clamming up." He moved toward her as he undid his tie and tossed it on the bed. "I care about you more than I thought I'd ever care about a woman. You've met my ex. After breaking off things with her, after feeling traumatized by her, I vowed to stay away from serious relationships. She's enough to make a man consider priesthood for the rest of his life."

Antika laughed and agreed. "Yeah, she is a bit...much."

"This...this thing developing between us wasn't supposed to get this far. We were supposed to go on a few dates, and then return to our singleness," he said, using her word. "I'm sorry for complicating everything, but...I like you. A lot."

Antika's pulse amped at his admission and knew it didn't come easy for him. Like her, he'd been hurt. But unlike him, she had never spent a night in jail because someone betrayed him.

The biggest problem right now was that her feelings for him were much stronger than his were for her. She could admit, to herself in this moment, that she wanted him in every way a woman wanted a man. But their feelings weren't mutual.

Maybe not yet, but it could happen, a voice inside her head boomed—one that sounded too much like Tamera. Antika shook the thought free. She didn't feel like thinking about anything, but decisions needed to be made.

"Where do we go from here?" she asked.

He sat beside her, his leg brushing up against hers and sending a thrill through her body. She wanted to scream. She wanted to tell him how she felt, but she'd been vulnerable enough in past relationships. She had to do a better job protecting herself, but how?

She wanted what she wanted. *Him.*

He reached for her hand and linked their fingers. "Do you want us to end this...to go back to being single the way we've vowed to do? Because if you do, I'll start the rumors going that you broke up with me. That you think we'll be better as friends. But that's not what I want right now. I want to keep going with this. I want to still be your plus one for your work event."

Antika stared down at their joined hands, and her pulse raced.

She wanted to be with him, in any capacity, more than she wanted anything else. But could she risk getting hurt in the end? Because the longer they continued this charade, the harder it would be to walk away.

She glanced at him, and the sincerity she saw in his eyes stabbed her in the chest. She loved when he looked at her with such intensity.

"I want what you want," she said quietly, but deep down, she wanted more.

So much more.

She touched his beard, running her fingers over its softness, then leaned in and covered his mouth with hers. She loved kissing him. Loved the way he slid his arm around her waist and pulled her against his body the way he was doing now. And she loved the way he made her feel precious. Desired. Cherished.

Antika might've started the kiss, but Drevon quickly took over.

He kissed her with a hunger that matched the fire burning inside of her. She didn't know what the future held for them, but she was going to enjoy every minute of the time they had together.

Starting now.

Chapter Twenty-Two

ine.

The word blasted through Drevon's head and almost knocked him off kilter, shaking him to his core as he loved on Antika's sensuous mouth. With a few misplaced words, he had almost ruined the best thing that had ever happened to him—meeting her.

She was important to him. He could admit that, but that moment outside of the restaurant, he had almost said more than he was ready to admit. Right now, though, he wanted to put all thoughts aside and just feel.

Drevon eased her back on the bed and partially covered her body with his as he deepened the kiss.

Mine.

There it was again. That small word that meant so much. Drevon had never claimed a woman as his own before, but that's how strongly he felt for Antika. He wasn't sure what to do with this new revelation, but he planned to show her how much he desired her in every way possible.

Antika fisted the front of his shirt, inadvertently pulling

him even closer. He loved how bold she was getting with him, and he wanted her just as bad. But right now, he wanted to do more than just kiss her.

When he slowly eased his mouth from hers, she groaned in protest. Drevon smiled as he sat up and pulled her up with him.

"Yesterday, I didn't give you the proper tour of everything in my condo," Drevon said against her lips before breaking off the kiss. "How about we explore my huge shower?"

Antika's mouth dropped open. *"Together?"*

He laughed. "Yeah together. Come on. Come and shower with me."

She nibbled on her bottom lip, and his dick shifted. Everything about this woman turned him on, and he was even more attracted to her because she didn't even realize her sexiness.

"I'll admit the shower is a good size, but it didn't look big enough to hold two people."

"Well, it'll do for what I have in mind." He winked, then stood.

He toed off his shoes, kicking them aside while undoing the gemstone cufflinks, then he placed those on a tray on his dresser. Next, he unbuckled his belt, pulled the tail of his shirt out of his pants, then started unbuttoning it. All the while he kept his attention on her, even when he tossed the shirt on the bed.

Yearning flooded through him as Antika swallowed hard. Her greedy gaze zoned in on his chest and abs, making him glad he worked overtime to stay in good physical shape. Next, he unzipped his pants, let them slide down his legs, then kicked them to the side.

Her heated gaze went lower and the hungry look in her eyes had his dick growing harder. He was hard enough to punch a hole through his boxer briefs. So he went ahead and stepped out of them.

"Now, your turn," he said.

"I've never showered with a man before...but if I'm going to have a first, I want it with you."

His heart thudded noisily inside his chest. "Damn, baby. When you say stuff like that, it makes me want you even more. Now strip."

After a slight hesitation, she turned her back to him, and he unzipped her black cocktail dress, peppering kisses along her scented neck and shoulders in the process.

Wanting to watch her strip for him, Drevon took a step back because there was no way he'd be able to keep his hands off her. The dress did a slow crawl down her curvaceous body and landed in a puddle around her ankles. She unfastened her lacy bra then turned to face him, and his mouth watered as she slipped it off.

Damn. She had the most beautiful breasts. Full, round, and way more than a handful. Just the way he liked. He itched to cup them, lick them, and suck on them until she screamed his name.

But she distracted him and was clearly getting into character as she struck a pose. Hair piled on top of her head, an hourglass figure, and shapely legs that seemed to go on forever. She looked like a fucking African goddess, all statuesque...and absolutely stunning.

She knew the affect she was having on him while she stood before him half naked. A vision, a fantasy come to life. His need to have her in his arms and be buried balls-deep inside of her was almost overwhelming.

Her large breasts with her nipples standing at attention, combined with the sexy black lace panties, had his heart hammering against his ribs. He wanted to touch her, wanted to devour every inch of her lush body, but he was rooted in place, unable to rip his eyes from her.

One of her hands rested on her rounded hip, while she held the other one up with her bra dangling from her fingertips. She stood that way for a few seconds, then grinned and dropped the garment to the floor.

Drevon's need for her multiplied as he approached her, desire charging through his body. "No matter how often I see your gorgeous body it still makes me drool."

Antika laughed and with his assistance, finished getting undressed.

When they finally made it to the bathroom, his dick throbbed to the point of aching. He wanted to take his time, wanted her to enjoy this experience, but he wanted her so bad. It was going to take herculean strength not to plunge right into her.

He reached into the glass enclosure and turned on the water while she grabbed a shower cap from her toiletry bag on the counter. Again, she nibbled on her lips as if debating on whether to put it on. Surely, she didn't think a white shower cap would discourage his desire for her.

"Put it on," he said and grabbed a condom from one of the drawers. When they climbed into the shower, he set it on the ledge next to his shower gel.

No words were spoken. None were needed as they stood under the water spray watching each other. Drevon cupped her cheek, and emotion clogged his throat as he stared into her eyes. Feelings he had never felt and still didn't want to put a name to swirled inside of him.

This woman. This incredibly beautiful woman had charged into his life and made it better without even trying. He'd do anything for her. But right now, all he wanted to do was love on her.

He moved her slightly to the right and backed her against the tiled wall. Linking his fingers with hers, he lifted both her arms over her head.

"You're important to me," he said and kissed her lips. "You have made the last few weeks some of the best of my life." He kissed her cheek. "And your body is truly a gift from God for my pleasure."

She laughed, and he smiled before he started dotting kisses over her cheek, down her neck and against her throat.

He held her arms above her head with one hand and used his other to cup her breast before he lowered his head and pulled a taut nipple into his mouth. He sucked, teased, and swirled his tongue around the harden peak, loving the erotic sounds coming from her as she wiggled against him.

"Dre," she whined, and that only spurred him on more.

He moved to her other breast, working her into a frenzy as he sucked her hard. When his teeth grazed her sensitive nipple, she cried out and bucked against him.

A grin kicked up the corners of his mouth.

Yeah, she was almost ready for him.

Without releasing the nipple that was between his teeth, he let go of her arms and her hands flew to the back of his head. She held on to him while he continued sucking, licking, loving on her succulent body. Then he squeezed her breasts together and continued feasting on them.

He couldn't get enough. He smothered his face between her large mounds as he tweaked and stroked her nipples. The scent of her lovely perfume tickled his nose, and he burrowed his face even deeper.

"Dre—Drevon," she panted roughly, her hips bucking against him.

"Hmm," he moaned, but made no move to stop the sweet torture he was inflicting on her.

"I need you. I want you now," she cried.

Hearing her begging for more of him made his dick harder. She was nearing her release, and he wanted to be buried deep inside of her when that happened.

Drevon lifted his head and kissed his way back up her voluptuous body until he reached his full height. Antika's arms went around his neck seconds before she kissed him like a starving woman devouring a turkey sandwich.

Damn, this woman knew how to turn him on, and he couldn't wait any longer to be inside of her. Dragging his mouth from hers, he grabbed the condom and quickly sheathed himself. His dick throbbed, and even more so when she spread her legs, inviting him in. Drevon wasted no time sliding between her slick folds.

His mouth found hers again, but his thoughts fragmented as he started thrusting into her, and she moved with him stroke for stroke. He barely noticed the water pelting down on them as they melded together as one.

"*Shiiit*, you feel so damn good," he mumbled against her mouth, but when she lifted one of her legs and wrapped it around him, pulling him in deeper, Drevon almost lost it.

He ripped his mouth from hers and held her leg up as he thumped into her like a man possessed. He couldn't help it. With each thrust, Antika gave as good as she got. He relished every sound she made, and the way she touched and held on to him was almost too much.

She was too much, but Drevon couldn't stop driving into her even if he wanted to.

He released her leg and gripped her hips, struggling to hang on while her sex pulsed around his dick, squeezing him so tight he almost lost his breath.

"That's it. That's it," she panted as he kept driving into her. "That's it."

Every time she screamed out filled his passion and made him go harder. Faster.

"Yes. Yes. Dre! *Yesss!*"

Her nails dug into his shoulders as she bucked wildly against him, chasing her orgasm when suddenly she cried out. Screaming his name over and over until she surrendered to her release.

Drevon loved watching her fall apart, and within seconds, a hot wave of passion raged through his body and launched him over the proverbial edge of his control.

Chest heaving, he collapsed against Antika, pressing her against the tiled wall and probably holding her too tight as he struggled to catch his breath.

They stood there, body limp, knees weak, and panting heavily near each other's ears. Even when the water started to cool, it took them a while before either could move.

Drevon blew out an exhausted breath then finally lifted his head. "You okay?" he asked, and his heart flipped inside his chest when a sensual smile graced her lips.

"Better than okay."

She kissed him so sweetly, and in that moment, Drevon knew he was all the way gone.

Chapter Twenty-Three

Drevon stood on Jet's doorstep, waiting for him to open the door. He could hear Rocky, Jet's two-year-old boxer, barking on the other side of the threshold. He'd been debating with himself for the last three days since returning from New York on whether to talk to his boys about Antika. Even with them checking in a few times, texting back and forth on stuff, he hadn't really shared much about her since telling them about the engagement.

Today, though, he needed to hash it out with someone and determine next steps with her.

Jet might not be the best sounding board—mainly because he wasn't looking to fall in love and settle down, especially no time soon. Yet, he lived the closest.

What the hell is taking him so long? Instead of ringing the bell again, Drevon pounded on the door.

They all had keys to each other's houses, but after Montez walked into Jet's house one morning when he had a woman there, they all decided that ringing the doorbell was a must.

"What's up, Dre?"

Drevon whirled around, surprised to see his cousin.

"Not much," he said, and they gave each other a fist bump. "What's up with you?"

"Nothing, but why aren't you answering your phone? I just left you a message to see what you were up to."

Before Drevon could respond, the barking stopped, and the door swung open. Jet, wearing a wrinkled T-shirt and sweatpants, looked as if he hadn't slept in days. While he held on to Rocky's collar, his gaze bounced between Drevon and Montez.

"What is this, some type of intervention?" he asked dryly and opened the door wider for them to enter.

"It wasn't but should it be?" Drevon asked, giving his friend another once-over before strolling into his townhome. "You look like hell, man."

"You should talk. Your ass don't look that great, either," Jet said, following behind them. "Wait. Dre, if you're here looking like someone kicked your puppy, that means you must be having woman problems."

They knew each other too well. It was almost scary, and if Jet's appearance was any indication, they both might be having issues on the same subject.

Drevon couldn't speak for him, but what he was feeling these days about Antika was nothing like anything he'd ever dealt with in his life.

Something had shifted between him and his *fiancée* during their trip. Something he didn't know how to fix. He had come back a different man, and now he had to figure out how to move forward.

"What's it going to be tonight, boys?" Jet asked, and pointed into his dining room where he had a dining table that easily converted to a pool table. It had to be one of the top ten greatest inventions. "We shooting pool, or are we going to make all of our issues disappear with liquor?"

"I vote liquor." Drevon kept walking until he reached the kitchen. "I can't handle you guys kicking my ass in pool tonight."

His ego wouldn't be able to deal with it. His pool game was all right, but Jet and Montez were better. Now, had it been golf or basketball they were going to play, he could give them a run for their money.

"Fine. We can drink, and I'll see if I can help you two with whatever the hell is going on with you," Montez said and sat on the bar stool next to Dre while Jet went to the other side of the counter.

Drevon petted Rocky behind the ears before the dog ambled away to his doggy bed.

"I assume tequila is okay," Jet said and pulled three shot glasses from the cabinet. He lined them up on the granite before grabbing the liquor bottle. Based on the label on the bottle, it was the good stuff.

Great. Dre wasn't in the mood for any watered-down crap.

Once the glasses were filled, they all grabbed one and held it up. Neither said a word, just clinked them together and tossed the liquor back.

They all cringed as the alcohol slid down their throats, coughing and grunting as they slammed the glasses on the counter.

"Damn, man. That stuff seems stronger than usual," Montez choked out, then cleared his throat. "What did you do, add gasoline to it?"

As they laughed, some of the tension eased from Drevon's shoulders. Small talk flowed easily as they discussed everything and nothing. They'd all had a couple of busy weeks, but somehow found time to spend with the women in their lives.

"I think I'm in love with Antika," Drevon said without preamble, and threw back another shot of tequila.

He slammed the glass down and pointed for Jet to refill it. He wasn't planning to get drunk, but it was probably a good idea that he had used a car service to get to Jet's place. He needed to knock the edge off, because the emotions swirling inside of him were driving him nuts.

"On top of that, this stupid engagement feels like I'm stuck in a straitjacket with no way of getting out of it without breaking my arms."

Montez's eyebrows dipped into a frown. "What the hell does that even mean?"

"Antika insists that after her company's event in a couple of weeks, she wants us to call off the engagement. I'm not sure if I'm ready. It'll be a lose-lose for both of us in one way or another. The plan is to tell people the engagement is off because we realize that we're better as friends and so we decided not to get married."

Jet shrugged. "Does that mean you gon' have a broken engagement party?" Jet asked just before he threw back a shot, and Drevon and Montez glared at him.

Their friend was always the type to use jokes to mask fear, pain, and even insecurity, and sometimes that same humor showed up at inopportune moments.

"Man, what's wrong with you?" Montez asked. "Did you not hear him say he was in love with Antika?"

"Yeah, I heard him." Jet propped his hip against the kitchen counter and folded his arms across his chest. "But if she doesn't love you back, you need to walk before you're the one getting hurt."

Drevon studied his friend, who really did look as if he hadn't slept in a few days. He watched as Jet poured another drink. "Are we talking about me, or you?"

Jet stared down at the counter for the longest time, then

huffed out a breath before looking up. "We're talking about you."

Drevon was fairly sure he was lying. He didn't know what was going on with his friend, but he'd figure it out before they parted ways.

"Do you think she loves you?" Montez asked.

"I think she has strong feelings for me, but we're both afraid to be vulnerable. I've always said that I'll never get married. Bachelor for life. But...I'm not sure about that anymore. And Antika's been hurt one too many times. She doesn't want anything serious for fear she'll get hurt again. What if we give our relationship a try and I hurt her?"

"What makes you think you will?" Jet asked. "If you love her and you think the feeling is mutual, why are you holding back? Why not go for what you want?"

"I've never been in love before. I might screw it up. Or what if I pour my heart out to her, and she turns me down?"

Jet and Montez didn't respond. Instead, they both looked deep in thought. Especially Jet who appeared lost in his own issues.

Yep, they were absolutely going through the same thing...at the same time.

"This is going to be a long night," Jet muttered, and refilled their glasses.

"You need to tell her how you feel, and then beg her to give you a chance to prove that she's the one for you," Montez insisted. He started to say more but his phone vibrated in his pocket, and he pulled it out, then smiled. "Well, fellas, I need to go." He headed to the door.

"Where you going?" Jet called out.

"To see Desiree. Unlike you two, I don't have woman problems. So think about what I said—both of you. I'm out."

"I hate to admit it, but Montez's advice might be on point."

Jet lifted one of the glasses and Drevon did the same. "Here's to proving our love to the women in our lives."

"I'll drink to that."

Drevon tossed back the liquor wondering how he could convince Antika to take a chance on him.

Chapter Twenty-Four

I'm in love with Drevon Ross.

    It wasn't infatuation. It wasn't a crush. It wasn't lust, but it was crazy. How could she have let this happen? Their engagement was fake. Yet, somehow she had let her stupid heart get involved.

Gawd! I knew this would happen.

She had the bad habit of falling for the wrong guys. Except this time, she'd fallen for the most amazing, encouraging, fun-loving wrong guy. A man who she loved, but one who would break her heart.

"Welcome to my home, Antika."

She turned and smiled at one of Battle Brigade's owners. "Thank you, Mr. Leonard, and thanks for hosting the gala tonight. Your home is beautiful," she said, but beautiful wasn't a strong enough word to describe the luxurious estate.

"Thank you, and it's our pleasure to celebrate all of you tonight, and I heard about your engagement. Congratulations."

"Thank you," she said around the lump in her throat. She was so tired of living a lie.

"Where's this fiancé of yours that my wife has been going on and on about?"

Antika smiled. She and Drevon had arrived fifteen minutes ago to the Battle Brigade's All-Star Event, and the first person they ran into was his wife. Of course, Drevon had charmed her within minutes.

She nodded toward the double doors that led out to a massive patio overlooking a man-made lake. "He had to take an important call."

"Well, be sure to introduce us before the end of the night."

"I will, sir."

"In the meantime, have a good time."

As he strolled away, Antika snagged a glass of champagne from one of the passing servers. Some walked around with trays of drinks, while others had platters of hors d'oeuvres.

Antika's gaze went to the patio doors where Drevon stood just beyond them. She marveled at how good he looked tonight. His hair and beard were perfectly groomed, and it was as if he was born to wear a tuxedo. It highlighted his broad shoulders that tapered down to a narrow waist and made him look ten feet tall. He was gorgeous.

As if sensing her watching him, he turned toward her and flashed that smile that always made her nipples pebble and her body vibrate with need. This was their last night together and her heart ached knowing that they'd soon be going their separate ways. But she wanted him more than she wanted her next breath.

What would he say if she told him that she changed her mind, that she didn't want to walk away from him?

"You might as well stop gawking at the man," a familiar voice said from behind her, and Antika cringed. "He's so far out of your league. It's only a matter of time before he dumps you."

"Go to hell, Edward, and I mean that. *Go. To. Hell*," she

emphasized, not bothering to look back at him. Instead, she glanced around the magnificent ballroom, waving at a few coworkers across the room.

"I hate to admit it, but you look nice tonight."

"Thank you," she said, brushing a hand down the side of her royal-blue, halter-top backless cocktail dress that brought attention to her full breasts. Drevon had helped her pick out the outfit during their shopping trip while in New York. Considering how much attention he always gave her breasts and her legs, she wanted a dress that would highlight both. The garment stopped mid-thigh, and she had paired it with stiletto sandals in the same color.

"I was thinking..." Edward started and gripped her elbow.

Antika flinched. She jerked away from him more out of reflex than anything else. He had barely touched her, but she'd prefer to keep distance between them.

"Touchy, touchy," he said, a little too close to her ear. His hot breath against her skin was unwelcome. "There was a time when you liked me touching you."

"Maybe, but now it feels like a thousand ants scurrying over my skin," she retorted. "Keep your hands to yourself. Otherwise, be prepared to lose one."

Edward chuckled. "Good one," he said, and Antika was surprised he didn't say more. Normally, he did, but maybe he planned to be on his best behavior this weekend.

"Hey, baby. Sorry about that. My call ran longer than intended," Drevon said as he slipped an arm around her waist and pulled her against his side.

Ahh, maybe Edward saw Drevon coming over and that's why he didn't engage in their usual verbal sparring.

Antika leaned into Drevon, and his alluring scent wrapped around her like a cashmere blanket. When she gazed up at him, the heated look he was giving her made her heart jolt and her panties damp.

Damn him for making her want him.

"You doing okay?" he asked quietly.

"I'm great." Antika slid her arm around his waist and covered his mouth with hers. It was only supposed to be a little peck, but Drevon had other ideas.

He nudged her lips apart with his tongue and kissed her like she was the sweetest thing he'd ever tasted. As his tongue tangled with hers, he held her close, and she moaned. She moaned, not caring that there were people around.

How was she going to survive without him in her life? Without his touch and his addictive kisses? Her self-esteem might've taken a hit after Edward but spending time with Drevon had mended the broken pieces of her heart.

"Enough already. We get that you're in love," Edward said on a humorless laugh.

Antika wanted to growl, and Drevon actually did. His eyes searched hers, and she was pretty sure they were thinking the same thing—*I want to get you naked.*

Drevon turned to Edward. "I would say it's nice to see you again, but I'd be lying." He moved closer. "If you ever put your hands on her again, I'll break your damn fingers."

Antika's mouth dropped open at the lethal tone behind his words, but shut it quickly.

Gone was the pretty boy that she had met weeks ago, and in his place was someone she didn't recognized. He seemed taller. He seemed broader and hell, he seemed to have morphed into a man who could back up his words.

She glanced at Edward, and Antika almost laughed at his shocked expression. He had bully tendencies, but right now, he looked like a chump who had just got his ass handed to him.

Good. If she was lucky, he'd stay the hell away from them for the rest of the night.

"Hi, honey. Sorry I'm late," a pretty, redheaded woman said when she reached Edward. Then she looked from him to Drevon, then back to Edward.

But then she did a double take at Drevon. "Hey, you're that model, Drevon Ross, aren't you?"

"Yes," he said, and just then, an announcement for everyone to find their table came through the speakers. "If you two will excuse us."

Drevon escorted Antika to their table, and she was glad to learn that Edward was not sitting with them.

Thank God.

Chapter Twenty-Five

"**F**inally, a moment alone," Drevon said as he and Antika stood on the patio looking out over the lake.

Surprisingly they had the area to themselves. Most people were inside enjoying the live band and the open bar. Dinner had been great, and the award ceremony was nice, too, but he was ready to leave. She wasn't.

He placed a kiss on her bare shoulders. "Did I tell you how stunning you look?"

She turned in his arms to face him and smiled as she slid her arms around his waist. His heart squeezed as he stared into her eyes.

"You might've mentioned it a few times, and I must say, you're looking pretty dapper yourself."

Drevon didn't know what she was thinking, but he was thinking that it was time to tell her how he felt. The problem was, she'd made him promise not to talk about their future until after the event.

They might've gotten together under unusual circumstances, but there was no doubt in his mind that she was his. He

155

just had to convince her. For now, he'd make sure she never wanted to leave him.

"You make a great fake boyfriend."

He grinned and gave her a quick peck on the lips. "What can I say? That's what you're paying me for."

The moment the words slid from his mouth Drevon knew he had screwed up.

She stiffened in his hold, and hurt flashed in her eyes, but just as quickly, it disappeared. In its place was sadness.

Shit, I'm an idiot!

"Baby, I'm sorry," he hurried to say, but Antika pushed against his chest to get out of his hold. "We are way past the way things started between us."

When he didn't immediately release her, she said, "Let me go."

There was no anger in her voice. She didn't curse his stupid, insensitive ass out. She didn't even raise her voice, which only elevated her classiness in his eyes.

A low growl bubbled inside of him, and Drevon reluctantly dropped his arms from around her, but he stayed close.

"Tika, I didn't mean—"

"No," she said and touched his arm before snatching her hand back. "You're right. I'm being silly. This was just a job for you, and we got carried away. I'm going to freshen up, and then we can leave."

"Antika..." He reached for her hand just as she started to turn, and he was glad she didn't pull away. "I am so sorry. I shouldn't have said that."

"No apology necessary." She smiled, but it didn't reach her eyes as she eased out of his hold before turning away.

Drevon punched the air hard enough to throw out his shoulder, then turned back to the lake. How stupid could he be? Why'd he bring up the damn arrangement, especially considering he'd temporarily forgotten about it?

He ran his hand over his low haircut. "I'm an idiot."

I have to fix this.

"I knew something was shady between you two."

Drevon whirled around and saw Edward in the shadows, leaning against the house. Two tall bushes were slightly concealing him. He moved forward, swaying slightly with a drink in his hand. He tossed back the dark liquor, then threw the glass in the bushes behind him.

I knew something was shady between you two. Edward's words played on a loop inside Drevon's mind. The guy might be tipsy, but not too drunk to hear what they'd said.

Shit. This is bad.

Drevon debated on how to play this. Maybe he could convince the asshole that he hadn't heard correctly.

Before he could try and reason with the guy, Edward spoke again.

"I *think*," he said, drawing out the word, "that people might want to know that your pretty face is a fake," he spat and bumped into another tree, then shook his head. "No, that's not right. The engagement is fake."

Unease clawed through Drevon, and he slowly approached the guy, careful to keep some space between them. He didn't trust himself not to knock his ass out.

Edward continued speaking. "After I tell everyone, then I'm getting Antika back."

Drevon didn't even feel himself move. All he knew was one minute they were standing in the middle of the patio, and the next, his hands were fisted in the front of Edward's shirt. He slammed him against the house.

"Man, don't fuck with me," he ground out close to Edward's ear and held him in place with a forearm on the man's neck. "Don't let this pretty face fool you. Step to my woman, or say *anything* about what you *think* you heard, and I will make your life a living hell. Try me and see what happens."

Drevon might not have been a fighter, but few knew that he had taken karate from the time he was three years old through high school. He stopped before getting his black belt, but he still could hold his own.

He tightened his grip, ignoring the way Edward grasped and clawed at his arm. "Do I make myself clear?"

"Yes," Edward rasped. "Yes," he said again before Drevon jerked his arm away and watched the bastard stumble forward before righting himself.

They locked eyes and neither said a word when a small group of people came out on the patio.

Drevon started to follow Edward inside but a couple of the women who were now outside asked him to take a picture with them.

He groaned internally but obliged.

At least it would give him time to come up with what to say to Antika, because *I love you* might not be enough.

Asshole.

Bastard.

Jerk.

Those were only a few appropriate names to describe her fiancé for hire as she stood in front of the bathroom mirror. She rubbed her chest as if that would help the ache in her heart.

I quit. I should've stuck with my initial plan—embrace my singleness.

As emotions swirled inside of her and she thought about

the incredible man who'd been her fake fiancé for weeks, tears filled her eyes.

But she bit down on her bottom lip, refusing to shed a single one. She wouldn't cry. She had no intention of ever crying over a man again.

Huffing out a breath, Antika lowered her gaze and leaned on the vanity. Drevon had ruined everything by bringing up their arrangement.

Granted, he wasn't wrong. She had hired him, but somewhere along the way, she had forgotten about that. Now it was thrown back in her face.

"This is pitiful on so many levels," she mumbled under her breath. She had vowed that she would never let another man make her feel less than or unworthy. Though Drevon made her feel like a precious gift, his words reminded her of how desperate she'd been to have a man in her life, even temporarily.

This is on me. This is all on me.

She wasn't mad at him. She loved him, and that's what had her feeling worse than anything.

Damn him for making me fall in love with his fine ass.

The whole situation was sad. But at least he had helped her do what she'd set out to do, taunt Edward. Show him that she had moved on to bigger and better.

But walking away from Drevon wasn't going to be easy. She knew that he'd been joking a few minutes ago, but it wasn't funny that she paid someone to go out with her. His words had felt like a big bucket of ice water had been poured over her head, drenching her in self-pity.

Might as well get this over with.

Antika swung open the bathroom door and pulled up short. There he was leaning against the wall, looking sexier than any man had a right to look. He was staring at her, sorrow in his eyes.

He pushed away from the wall. "Baby, I'm so sorry, and I need you to hear me out. Okay?"

Instead of responding, she nodded because she didn't trust herself to speak. Not when emotion clogged her throat.

"I didn't mean to make you feel bad about how we got together. Actually, I should've told you this sooner, but I asked my aunt to cancel the contract."

"What?" Surprise coursed through Antika. "When?"

He pulled his cell phone from his pants pocket and scrolled through his text messages before he lifted his phone up for her to read the screen. "It was right before Tamera's party."

Drevon: *Cancel Antika's contract. Refund her money. I'll cover any fees. I like her. I'm planning to get to know her better —without a contract over our heads.*

Aunt Vi: *I knew it! I knew the moment I met her that she'd be perfect for you. I'm taking full credit when you two get married.*

Antika snorted at the last part. She didn't really know Mrs. Ross, but the woman seemed like a trip.

"I know our relationship started out a bit unusual," Drevon continued, "but that didn't stop me from falling in love with you."

She gasped, shocked that he'd said the words that she'd longed to hear from him.

He smiled. "Yeah, *I love you.* If I wasn't such a punk, I would've told you while we were in New York, but this is new territory for me. So I'm sure I'm going to mess up along the way, but Antika, I need you to know that you mean everything to me."

"Oh, Dre," she said, her hand over her heart and a rogue tear sliding down her cheek.

He cupped her face between his hands and with the pads of his thumb, he swiped away a few more tears that slipped through. "I love you so damn much."

"I love you, too," she said, gripping the front of his jacket.

He lowered his head and kissed her. His lips were so soft and gentle that she felt his love flow through her from the top of her head to the soles of her feet.

This moment felt like a dream. A dream come true.

When the kiss ended, Drevon lowered his forehead to hers. "How about we get out of—"

His phone rang, and he almost ignored it, but he pulled it from his pocket and glanced at the screen. A slow grin spread across his face, then he turned the phone so Antika could see who was calling.

Ryan Coogler.

"Oh, my goodness, Dre!" she squealed, doing a little happy dance. "You have to answer it." Ryan Coogler was his first choice of people to direct his movie.

"Answer it before he hangs up, and I'll meet you near the entrance." She gave him a quick kiss before setting out to say goodbye to a few people.

The music was louder the closer she got to the ballroom, but just as she started around the corner, Edward ran into her. She stumbled back, bumped into the wall, and shrieked when his liquor splattered onto the front of her dress.

"Damn it, Edward! Watch where you're going!" Anger charged through her as she feverishly wiped the alcohol from her dress, pissed that it would probably stain.

He put the glass on the floor and bumped into the wall but righted himself. "You're the—the person I—I'm looking for," he said, his words slurring as he crowded her.

"Edward, I'm not doing this with you tonight. You're drunk. Get away from me. Go bother your girlfriend."

He laughed and swayed. "You paid the model." His offensive breath made her lean back until she realized what he'd said and froze. "I—I knew. No—no way he—he'd be with you. You—you're mine anyway."

Antika was still stuck on *you paid the model*. Had he heard them on the patio?

"Edward, what are you talking about?"

He leaned in to kiss her, and she recoiled. "Ugh! Get away from me!" she yelled and pushed him, but he pinned her to the wall. "Edward, move!"

"What the hell?" Drevon roared, appearing out of nowhere. He jerked Edward away, practically lifting him off his feet before throwing him to the ground. "I told you to stay away from her!"

He slammed his fist into Edward's face, and Antika screamed. "Dre!"

She tried grabbing him, but two big guys barreled toward them.

"Hey! What's going on back here?" They yanked Drevon off Edward who had blood oozing from his nose.

"Let me go! That bastard attacked my fiancée!" Drevon jerked out of their grasp. His frantic gaze bounced around until it landed on Antika, and he rushed to her. "You okay? Did he hurt you?"

"No, I'm fine," she said, her heart pounding hard enough to beat out of her chest.

Apparently, Drevon wasn't convinced. His hands roamed over her body as if to make sure for himself that she was okay.

"Their en—engagement is fake. Liars!" Edward yelled as security carried him away. "She's mine! Not his!"

People filled the hallway, including the owners of the house, and Antika wished she could snap her fingers and disappear.

It was a complete circus. Thankfully no one believed Edward and assumed it was the liquor talking.

An hour later, she and Drevon stepped out into the hot muggy evening air to wait for the valet to bring their vehicle around.

Antika released an exhausted breath. "What a night."

"Come here," Drevon said, wrapping his strong arms around her, and she snuggled against his chest. She couldn't think of any other place she'd want to be than in his arms.

"I can honestly say that there's never a dull moment with you around."

Drevon's laughter rumbled against her ear that was pressed against his chest, and she smiled.

"I love you so much," he whispered. "If you agree to marry me for real, I promise you a life of excitement."

Antika lifted her head and stared into his gorgeous eyes. "I'd love to marry you."

Grinning, he pressed his lips against hers, and his kiss sang through her veins.

Antika never knew she could be as happy as she was in that moment. And she couldn't wait to see what the future held for them.

Epilogue

T *hree months later...*

I think I'm pregnant.

I might be pregnant.

God, what if I'm pregnant?

The words volleyed inside of Antika's head as she paced the length of Drevon's massive bathroom. She had showed up at his place a few minutes ago for dinner where they planned to discuss their future. Getting married, her moving in with him next weekend, and the list went on and on.

Antika leaned a hip against the double vanity and stared at the rectangular box in her hand. She'd been carrying around the home pregnancy test for days, debating on when to take it. Her period was over a week late, but that could be due to the stress of her busy work schedule and all the changes in her life. Good changes but changes nonetheless.

The Monday after the fiasco at the Battle Brigade celebration, she'd been shocked to learn of Edward's resignation. The owner who'd been hosting the event had been livid by his behavior. He had apologized profusely to her and Drevon, assuring them that the matter would be dealt with and that she wouldn't have any more problems from Edward.

Antika later learned that Edward had been put on a behavior improvement probation months earlier after HR had received complaints regarding the way he talked to his subordinates. Then after his behavior the night of the event, he'd been given the option to resign or be terminated. He chose to resign.

What surprised Antika even more was when Edward called to apologize to her regarding his behavior during their relationship, but especially at work. That had been a first. He never apologized for anything. She half expected there to be a catch. Yet, he seemed sincere and had even wished her well. She hadn't heard from him since.

"Antika."

Antika startled at the sound of Drevon yelling up the stairs. She opened the bathroom door. "Yes?"

"Baby, dinner will be ready in ten minutes."

"Okay. I'll be down shortly."

Her attention went back to the pregnancy test. *It's now or never*. She read the instructions then took the test.

The last few months had been a whirlwind. Drevon's movie project had been green lighted, and he was thrilled, but also incredibly busy. Filming wouldn't start until the following year, but there was a ton of tasks to be handled prior to that. Thankfully, production would mostly be done in Atlanta.

Antika couldn't be happier for him...for them. He'd made sure to keep her in the loop on everything, which she appreciated. More than that, though, she loved how he put their relationship first when making decisions.

She glanced at the pregnancy test that now laid on a pile of toilet paper on the vanity. In a couple of minutes, she'd know - *pregnant* or *not pregnant.*

Her nerves were getting the best of her. It wasn't that she thought Drevon would leave her, but they hadn't talked about kids. They'd barely had time to discuss wedding plans. But she had turned forty last month. Her window of opportunity was closing quickly. So it felt like a now or never scenario even though she knew women still had babies in their forties.

She checked the time on her watch. *Times up.*

"Okay, here goes." She lifted the test from the vanity and stared at it.

Pregnant.

"Oh, my God. *Pregnant.*"

She wasn't sure how long she stood there staring at the word before she shook herself. She had to tell Drevon.

Trying to stop her hands from shaking, she wrapped the test in a wad of toilet paper, then washed her hands. Heart pounding, knees shaking, she finally left the bathroom and made her way down the stairs. All the while debating on how to tell the man she loved that they were having a baby.

We're having a baby. Part of her was thrilled, but the other part was freaking the hell out inside. When she reached the bottom step and turned the corner, Drevon glanced at her and smiled.

"Hey, I was thinking...but hear me out before you say no," he said, placing a pasta dish in the center of the banquette table. "I know it's been tough to pick a wedding date, but I want you as my wife. Since our engagement was spur of the moment, let's do the same with our wedding. Let's just do it. You're moving in next Saturday, how about we get married next Sunday?"

He lifted his hands out in front of him when she opened her mouth to speak.

"I know it's crazy, but neither of us want a big wedding. We'll have something nice, simple, and quick with our family and a few friends. We can have a light meal catered, have cake, and live happily ever after."

Antika's heart felt as if it would beat out of her chest. "Umm, okay."

Drevon set Italian bread and vegetables on the table then looked at her. At first, he was smiling, but then concern showed on his face. "What's wrong?" He hurried across the room to her and cupped her face between his large hands. "If you don't want to get married, I'll understand. As long as I have you, I—"

"I'm pregnant," Antika blurted. She whipped the test from behind her back and shoved it against his chest.

Drevon dropped his hands from her face and grabbed the blob of tissue just before it slipped from Antika's fingers. She swallowed hard as he stared down at the tissue as if afraid to see what was inside.

When his eyes finally met hers, it was as if he didn't recognize her.

Antika's heart sank. After things fell apart with Patrick, she had given up on the idea of having a family. But now her life was different. It was perfect. She had a man she adored, and she wanted this baby. More than anything, she wanted to raise this child with Drevon.

He pulled out the pregnancy test and stared at it. "You—you're pre—pregnant?" His gaze bounce from her face to her stomach and back to her eyes again that were now filling with tears. "Are you sure?"

"According to that stick in your hand, that claims to be ninety-nine percent accurate, yes."

More silence.

"Dre, I'm sorry. I'm not sure what or when—"

"Yes! Whew!" He roared and did a fist pump while leaping in the air then started walking aimlessly around the kitchen. "We're having a baby! *We're having a baby!*"

Antika covered her mouth with her hands and let her tears flow. Seeing him happy made her heart squeeze as excitement bubble inside of her.

As if suddenly remembering she was in the room, he rushed to her and wrapped her in a bear hug.

"After you agreed to be my wife for real, I didn't think I could get any happier." His deep voice was filled with emotion. He leaned back, cupped her face again, and shook his head. "Knowing that you're having my baby...Antika, I can't even express how happy that makes me. I love you so damn much, it feels like my heart is going to explode."

Antika swiped at her eyes and chuckled. "I know the feeling, and I love you too."

Drevon captured her lips in a heated kiss that made her toes curl, and joy surged through her body. She never knew she could experience such joy.

And to think, it all started with hiring a man.

Next Book in the Series

Thank you for reading Fiancé for Hire! If you enjoyed Drevon and Antika's story, consider leaving a review on review sites or social media outlets.

Also, be sure to check out the other books in the Men for Hire Series listed below.

BOYFRIEND FOR HIRE by Delaney Diamond
A one-night stand leads to much more...

Montez Ross's family owns At Your Service, a unique company that provides clients with men for both dating and handyman tasks. When the woman who left him after a one-night stand seeks their services, Montez, unaccustomed to being left, is annoyed but agrees to help her out.

Desiree Hagan is on track to make vice president of marketing at her firm but faces an obstacle: her terrible ex is her direct competition for the promotion. So she hires Montez to be her pretend boyfriend for an important company dinner which she doesn't want to attend alone. Now she has a new problem: unexpected feelings for Montez that she can't ignore.

DATE FOR HIRE by Reese Ryan

When former high school classmates unexpectedly reunite, will it be a second chance at romance with her unrequited crush?

When Amaya Walker hires a landscape designer, the last person she expects at her door is John Edward Thomas—her unrequited high school crush. Back then, she was the chubby book nerd who was often teased while he was the handsome heartbreaker who was out of her league. But now she's a big-shot creative director at a well-known recording label. And no one dare tease this plus-size diva who calls the shots and has learned to embrace her show-stopping curves. She'd like to keep nursing her grudge against Jet, but she's more attracted to him than ever.

Join Sharon's Mailing List

To get sneak peeks of upcoming stories and to hear about giveaways that Sharon is sponsoring, go to https://sharoncooper.net/newsletter to join her mailing list.

Other Books by Sharon C. Cooper

Atlanta's Finest Series

Vindicated (book 1)

Indebted (book 2)

Accused (book 3)

Betrayed (book 4)

Hunted (book 5)

Tempted (book 6)

Committed (book 7)

Jenkins & Sons Construction

Proposal for Love (book 2)

A Lesson on Love (book 3)

Unplanned Love (book 4)

Jenkins Family Series (Contemporary Romance)

Best Woman for the Job (Short Story Prequel)

Still the Best Woman for the Job (book 1)

All You'll Ever Need (book 2)

Tempting the Artist (book 3)

Negotiating for Love (book 4)

Seducing the Boss Lady (book 5)

A Love So Strong: A Jenkins Family Reunion (book 6)

Love at Last (Holiday Novella)

When Love Calls (Novella)

More Than Love (Novella)

Reunited Series

Secret Rendezvous (Prequel to Rendezvous with Danger)

Rendezvous with Danger (book 2)

Truth or Consequences (book 3)

Operation Midnight (book 4)

Casino Heat (book 5)

Standalones

Legal Seduction (Harlequin Kimani – Contemporary Romance)

Sin City Temptation (Harlequin Kimani – Contemporary Romance)

A Dose of Passion (Harlequin Kimani – Contemporary Romance)

Model Attraction (Harlequin Kimani – Contemporary Romance)

A Passionate Kiss (Contemporary Romance)

Soul's Desire (Unparalleled Love series)

Show Me (Irresistible Husband series)

His to Protect (Harlequin Romantic Suspense)

His to Defend (Harlequin Romantic Suspense)

Business Not As Usual (Romantic Comedy)

In It to Win It (Romantic Comedy)

Kiss Me (Irresistible Husband – Contemporary Romance)

Mr. One and Only (Baes of Juneteenth)

Fiancé for Hire (Men for Hire)

About the Author

USA Today bestselling author Sharon C. Cooper loves anything involving romance with a happily-ever-after, whether in books, movies, or real life. She writes contemporary romance, as well as romantic suspense and enjoys rainy days, carpet picnics, and peanut butter and jelly sandwiches. Her stories have won numerous awards over the years, and when Sharon isn't writing, she's hanging out with her amazing husband, doing volunteer work, or reading a good book (a romance of course). To read more about Sharon and her novels, visit www.sharoncooper.net